BAD MAGIC AND THE BIG TOP

BLACKWOOD BAY WITCHES MYSTERY BOOK 2

MISTY BANE

For Chris.
Du bist in meinem Herzen, du bist in meiner Seele

ALSO BY MISTY BANE

<u>Blackwood Bay Witches Mystery Series</u>

Haunted and Hexed (Book 1)

Bad Magic and the Big Top (Book 2)

Phantoms in High Fidelity (Book 3)

On A Witch and A Spell (Prequel Novelette)

Would you like to be notified of new releases and special offerings?

Stay in Touch!

Website

Facebook

Newsletter Sign Up

CHAPTER 1

$\mathcal{I}$'m sure there are worse ways to start the day than finding a dead clown on your doorstep, but I haven't personally experienced any. Okay, maybe I'm being a *tiny* bit dramatic. It wasn't actually my doorstep. I found him sitting on the concrete, slumped over against the bottom of the staircase that led up to the private entrance to my apartment.

I live in an old building right on the corner of Hemlock and Main Street in the middle of the cutest little old bay town in the Pacific Northwest. The lower level of the centuries old building is a bookstore and specialty shop called INVOKE and my apartment is just above it.

At first, I thought maybe the clown was just passed out. I wasn't really sure what clowns liked to do in their spare time, but drinking themselves into a stupor and passing out on sidewalks seemed a distinct possibility. But since he didn't budge when I nudged him with the toe of my Converse sneaker, I bit the bullet and decided to feel for a pulse. His skin was cold enough to the touch that I knew right away I wasn't going to find one; that was when I noticed the blood and the wad of paper stuffed in his mouth.

Even though I was in shock, and really creeped out, I did a quick scan of the area for his ghost. I didn't see him hanging around anywhere, so I figured he must've either wandered back to the circus or found his way into that great, bright light that everyone is always talking about.

Oh, I can see ghosts, by the way. It's one of the powers I have as a witch. I'd only just learned I was a witch when I'd inherited my grandmother's building *and* her magic and moved back to Blackwood Bay.

Already fishing my cell phone and keys out of my pocket, I ducked around to the front entrance of the shop to call the police. A column of sunlight stretched across the length of the floor and the distinct smell of a salty breeze tickled my nose; which was odd, because I had turned the lights off like I do every night and the bookstore always smelled like nothing but incense. But once I realized the back door—the one I lock up every night at closing—was very much unlocked and standing open, it was time to hightail it out of there.

"Are you okay, Dru?" Sergeant Wolf Harper asked. He was second-in-command at the small police station in town and also my Guardian. Apparently, every witch from the most powerful lines has one and, according to Granny, the Rathmores more than meet the requirements. I'd found out Harper was mine just a month prior, which complicated things a little since I may have had a tiny crush on him. Apparently, that was a huge no-no. Go figure.

"You look pale," he continued, concern in his piercing blue eyes.

"Well, aside from finding my shop broken into and a dead

body in front of my apartment this morning, clowns creep me out. You'd think he'd be less creepy since he's dead, but it's actually way worse. I keep expecting him to materialize right in front of me with a handful of red balloons and an evil laugh or something." I shuddered.

"So, I take it he's not still… around?" Harper lowered his voice.

I shook my head. "I don't see him and I'm really hoping he doesn't decide to come visit me later when I'm alone."

"Oh, but you're never alone," Harper teased. He was right. My grandmother's ghost kept me company. Since I'd been the sole heir of our family line of magic, Granny and I were stuck with each other until I learned everything I needed to and fully mastered my powers. At the rate things were going, I'd be an old spinster before I had any real privacy.

"I'm going to go out on a limb here and guess that he's probably with that traveling circus that came into town a few days ago?" My hair was long enough that my ponytail fell over my shoulder and I twirled it, catching a glimpse of deep red every few seconds. Most twenty-eight-year-olds don't have white hair, but it's made even more unique by the inch-long section of natural crimson color that's at the nape of my neck.

"Great detective work, assuming the clown is from the circus." Harper winked. He rolled his head from side to side and cracked his neck. "But I'm trying to figure out what a dead clown has to do with your store getting broken into last night. Did anyone at your place see or hear anything?"

Technically, I lived alone as I was the only living human— well, witch—but aside from Granny ghost, I also lived with my cat, Maui Lane, and my mother who had been living as a raven for the last twenty-eight years. Crazy story there. Anyway, another one of my powers I'd discovered was that I could communicate with animals. So when Harper asked if anyone saw or heard anything, he meant literally any soul—living or dead—that took up residence with me.

"No. I asked, but no one heard anything. That's pretty strange too, because the three of them are usually up at all hours. Granny doesn't sleep and she and Maui go back and forth all night while Mom tries to mediate. Then, of course, Trixie still pops in from time to time. It seems animals and ghosts don't really respect a person's need for sleep," I answered.

Harper nodded, looking thoughtful. "And you said nothing is missing?"

"Not that I can tell. I mean, I didn't take a full inventory or anything yet, but the cash register still has money in it. What else would someone steal from a weird store like this?" My recently inherited bookstore, as we commonly referred to it, was not the kind of bookstore you're thinking of. We sold everything from books on spells and charms to astral projection to wind chimes and incense. So much incense.

"I don't know, that four-foot gargoyle statue is pretty sweet," he joked.

"Excuse me, Officer?" A portly man approached, the sun bouncing off his balding head. On his arm was an older woman that could've easily passed for a Hollywood movie star straight out of the 1940s. Her blonde hair was curled away from her face, pinned back in swirling sections at the base of her neck. She wore a white fur draped around her shoulders and a matching white pencil dress. It was late summer in the Pacific Northwest, mind you, so we weren't exactly sweltering, but it was warm enough that I was comfortable in a tank top and shorts. I couldn't help but think the fur was less about comfort and more about appearances. She also carried one of those long cigarette holders and blew a slow puff of smoke from her lips.

"This is a crime scene, sir. You'll need to step back to the street," Harper said before turning to a group of officers loitering near a police cruiser. "Hey! Smith! Anderson! You two working today or should I put you both on unpaid leave? Where's the tape? Civilians are walking right up into our crime scene. Secure the scene! Knuckleheads." The two young officers both went pale before they started scurrying about, bumping into each other in an attempt to obey Harper's orders.

"I understand this is a crime scene, Officer." The portly man and his companion hadn't moved. "But that there is one of our own." He pointed to the deceased clown who had been haphazardly covered up, his curly red wig poking out above the sheet. "He went missing last night, and when we received a call from one of your officers this morning, even I couldn't have anticipated *this*."

"You're with the circus?" Harper asked.

"I am." The man held out his hand to Harper. "Marvin the Magnificent," he said proudly before motioning to the woman, "and this is the beautiful Elsa Braun."

"Charmed, I'm sure," the woman said in a faint German accent as she brought the cigarette to her lips. *Fancy.*

Harper shook the man's hand briefly before gesturing for them to move to the edge of the sidewalk near the street. I didn't exactly want to watch the police work or gape at the dead clown, so I stared down awkwardly at the sidewalk and strained to hear Harper's conversation. In my former life, the one I'd had right before I'd moved to Blackwood Bay, I'd been a private investigator for my dad's firm. Straining to hear other people's conversations was second nature because of the work I'd done. At least that was my excuse. Really, I was just nosy.

"Can you tell me who he is then?" I heard Harper ask.

"Yes, of course," Marvin answered. "His name was Chuckles."

"Chuckles? That doesn't sound like a real name," Harper said. I stole a glance to catch Marvin's response.

He shrugged and pulled a white handkerchief from his pocket to dab at his sweaty forehead. "It's the circus, sir. My name isn't really Marvin the Magnificent either."

"Okay." He had his back to me, but I was sure Harper was rolling his eyes. "We'll check his things and see if we can find some real identification. Tell me about Chuckles."

"He's been with us for nearly ten years now—"

"Sergeant!" an officer called out, interrupting. It was Dobson, Harper's right-hand man. He held up what looked like a cigarette butt, pinched carefully between the prongs of a pair of tweezers. I noticed there was a smudge of red on the tip, but I instantly recognized the thin purple band and emblem just above it.

Harper waved acknowledgment at Dobson before turning back to Marvin and Elsa. "Did Chuckles smoke?"

"Sure. In fact, many of our performers do. Every man has his vices, Officer." Marvin gave a tight smile.

"All right. What else can you tell me about Chuckles?"

"One of the finest acrobats you'd ever seen. Really such a loss." Marvin shook his head.

"He was an acrobat?" Harper asked.

"Yes," Marvin supplied without further explanation.

"Okay, I know you all arrived in town a few days ago, but you haven't had a show yet, correct? So why was Chuckles the acrobat dressed as a clown last night?"

"Oh, well, you see, we have a very special show. The acrobats and many of our other performers dress as clowns. You might even catch me wearing a red nose on Opening Night." Marvin gave a nervous laugh. "We do it to pay homage to our previous ringmaster. He always elected to forgo the typical ringmaster attire and dressed as a clown." Marvin smiled.

"My father," Elsa said flatly before she blew out a puff of smoke, her arm bent at the elbow and resting on Marvin's shoulder.

"Are you an acrobat too?" Harper addressed Elsa.

"Oh, heavens no." She smiled. "I'm terrified of heights."

"I see," Harper said and turned his attention back to Marvin, "but that still doesn't answer my question about why he was dressed as a clown *last* night."

"Oh, of course! I apologize." Marvin fidgeted with the handkerchief, ringing it between his hands. "I'm a bit out of sorts, as you can imagine. Last night was our final dress rehearsal, so everyone was in costume."

"Did Chuckles have an argument with anyone last night?"

"Pardon?" Marvin looked confused.

"Well, someone wasn't very happy with Chuckles, as you can see." Harper motioned to the lifeless clown.

"No, it wasn't one of us. I can assure you! We're a very tight-knit family. Any disagreements between us are quickly squashed."

"Did Chuckles have a lot of disagreements with your other performers?"

"No, that's not what I meant—" Marvin started.

"Officer," Elsa interrupted, "we all loved Chuckles. As Marvin said, he had his vices. He smoked, he drank far too much, and he liked to pay for his... *dates*, if you know what I mean, but he had a good heart. We're a family. For better or worse. You don't kill family."

"Well, we'll still be questioning everyone in your crew.

Please don't plan to leave town anytime soon."

"Oh, that's quite all right. We plan to stay as it is. We're still scheduled for another week of performances. Though I'm not sure how we'll replace Chuckles on such short notice."

"You're not shutting down the circus? At least for now?" Harper asked.

"Most certainly not. The show must go on. It's what Chuckles would've wanted. He truly was a performer at heart," Marvin said firmly.

"I see. Well, as you know, I have some officers already talking with your crew. And we'll need access to Chuckles' trailer. But I'll be in touch soon."

"Thank you. I want to do whatever I can to help find whoever hurt Chuckles." Marvin gave a small bow before holding out his bent arm for Elsa. She looped hers through his and gave a slight nod to Harper before letting Marvin lead her away.

Harper strode back over to me, scratching the five o'clock shadow on his chin, "Interesting characters, those two," he said.

"Circus folk." I shrugged. "I overheard your conversation—"

"Overheard?" Harper interrupted, "Or eavesdropped?"

"Whatever. Listen, that cigarette butt they found. That's a Tennessee King," I said excitedly.

Harper gave me a confused look.

"Sam, this guy that's worked for my dad since I was little, he used to smoke them. Years ago. He quit right after I started working at the PI firm, but I remember them well. Anyway, they're hard to find anymore—Sam had to drive to this special store to get them—but every pack has one cigarette with a joker emblem on the filter. It's supposed to be the lucky one in the pack."

Harper nodded, "Interesting. So if that cigarette butt doesn't belong to Chuckles, then we're looking for a clown killer that smokes joker cigarettes? Seems like a niche group."

"Right. Did Marvin say they aren't shutting down? At least for one night? It's gotta be an inside job, right? It's not like anyone in town would have a beef with a traveling circus clown."

"Whoa. Slow down, Little Miss *Former* Private Investigator." Harper studied me for a moment too long and I felt my cheeks flush.

"Don't 'little miss' me," I said, filling the silence. It was still difficult making prolonged eye contact with him. He had the most vibrant blue eyes I'd ever seen and sometimes I swore he could see right into my soul. Instead, I'd made a habit of either looking at the bridge of his nose or the cleft in his chin. It felt safer.

"Look, I'm inclined to agree with you." He placed his hands on his duty belt. "And I know you're smart and I'm sure you were very good at your old job, but why don't we both just... you know." He looked down at his feet and I could tell he was growing increasingly uncomfortable by the minute.

"No, I don't know. What do you mean?" I asked.

"I just mean, you let me handle the police work stuff and you handle the bookstore stuff."

"But the bookstore stuff is kind of boring. I mean, you know, compared to the thrill of solving murders and catching bad guys and stuff."

"Valid point, but not enough to deter me from reminding you to stay in your lane. It's safer there." His eyes finally met mine. "Why don't you tell me what this is really about?"

"What do you mean?" I feigned confusion.

"Dru, you love running the bookstore and spending time

with your friends all day. Also, the last time you got involved in one of my investigations, you almost got me killed, remember?"

"Hey, you're not special. I almost got, like, seven people killed," I joked.

He gave me a look and I knew he was waiting for a serious answer.

"Fine." I sighed. "Look, I want to help for two reasons. One, that poor man was murdered. And I'm a sucker for justice. Whoever killed him, they need to be caught. And it's possible that I can help."

"Mm-hmm… And the second reason?" He arched an eyebrow.

I lowered my voice. "Well, given that he was murdered, there's an extremely good chance that there's a ghost of a dead clown wandering around Blackwood Bay. And guess who he's most likely to come visit once he gets his bearings?" I jabbed a finger in my own direction. "I'd much prefer *we* find *him* and help him so he can be on his way sooner rather than later. I just want him to find his way into the great afterlife. And I want it done *before* he pays me an unexpected visit. I just… if I have to deal with him then I want it on my terms, Harper."

Harper cocked his head like he was considering it. "Clowns really scare you that bad, huh?"

"Come on, Harper. Don't tell me you couldn't use my skills. I'm a witch, remember? A witch that can communicate with ghosts. What better witness to a murder than the victim?"

He let out a dramatically long deep sigh. "I know, without a shadow of a doubt, that I'm going to regret this."

I couldn't keep from smiling.

"So, do you have any plans tonight?" He asked.

"Why?" I felt my heart leap.

"Because," he said, flashing me a cheeky little half smile, "I need a date to the circus."

CHAPTER 2

"I can't believe you lost your ring." Granny was pacing.

"Granny, I know. Look, it has to be around here somewhere." I checked my makeup for the hundredth time in the small mirror by the front door in my apartment.

"You can't just leave it lying around! Do you have any idea how important that ring is?" she lectured. I'd been given my mother's amber-colored ring when I was a baby and, although it wasn't the source of my magic, it boosted my powers and seemed to help me when I needed it most.

I groaned. "I know. I'm sorry. I'm so sorry. I'll find it. I promise."

"It was just an accident, Ma. Don't be so hard on her," my mother chimed in.

"Why weren't you wearing it anyway?" Granny asked.

"Because," I said, hurrying into the kitchen and beginning to furiously wipe down the countertop, "I get a little… swollen sometimes. Occasionally I'll take it off at night so I don't wake up with a finger that needs amputating."

"It's all those potato chips you eat before bed." Granny looked at me over the top of her glasses.

"Yes, I know. And you'll pry them out of my cold, dead fingers, so don't even try to convince me to give them up."

"Fine. But if you're going to take the ring off, you need a better system," she started again.

"Obviously," Maui purred in his flawless British accent from a spot on the couch.

"All right. I don't have time for this." I checked myself in the mirrored glass of the microwave before rushing to catch the timer on the oven. "Granny, I'll find it. I promise."

"Well, you'd better. Why are you baking right now, anyway?" She motioned to the pan of blueberry muffins sitting on the oven rack. "You're supposed to be leaving any minute."

"Because I'm nervous. I bake when I'm nervous."

"Huh. Interesting." She raised an eyebrow.

"What is?"

"You're not even a kitchen witch."

"What's a kitchen witch?" I asked, searching the drawers for a pot holder.

"Ma, you haven't told her what types of witches there are?" my mom asked.

"She's only been here a month, Aurora. I've been a little preoccupied trying to solve my own murder and then I needed a break," she said with a shrug of her shoulders.

"Granny, you weren't exactly trying to solve your murder alone." I laughed.

"No, but I did most of the heavy lifting."

Normally, I'd argue with her, but I was stressed enough as it was. "Anyway, since I'm not a kitchen witch, someone mind telling me what type I am?"

"You're an Endorn witch," Mom answered.

14

"An Endorn witch? What's that?" Finally, I found a pot holder shoved in the back of a drawer filled with packets of soy sauce, ketchup, and hot sauce. It was threadbare and had clearly seen better days, but I was already in a hurry.

"Well, in layman's terms, it basically means that with enough practice and knowledge, your power is limitless. You can do anything you want really," Granny said.

"Your magic isn't specialized. You can tap into any type you choose," Mom said.

"Endorn witches go back a very long way. To the very first witch," Granny said.

"But how did she get her magic?" I asked. "The very first witch, I mean." I pulled the muffin tin from the oven with my very old, very useless potholder and immediately felt the burning sensation radiate through my palm.

"Ah!" I dropped it onto the ground with a dramatic bang. "Rats!"

Maui sprang from the counter startled and let out a slew of curse words.

A sudden puff of blue smoke began to form, encompassing the metal tin. I opened my mouth to ask what was happening when two gray rodents scurried out from the spot where the muffin tin had landed. I shrieked, scrambling to get on top of the kitchen counter, my legs dangling in the air.

A low hiss came from Maui and he was off, a blur of black fur, chasing them around the apartment.

"Goodness sakes, girl. If I weren't already dead, you would've just scared the literal life out of me," Granny said above the ruckus.

"I'm terrified of rodents," I responded, my voice shaking.

"What are you, an elephant?" Granny jibed.

"What happened? Where did they come from?" I ignored her comment.

"Well, you lost your ring."

"What does that have to do with anything?"

"You're still coming into your magic. You'll get huge bursts and sometimes it will disappear completely. The ring helps keep it in balance until you're able to do it on your own. And since you lost it…"

"Since I lost it, what?"

"Your magic is bound to be a little… wonky," she said.

"Wonky? My magic is going to be wonky? What does that even mean?"

"It means when you dropped the muffin tin and said 'rats' your magic thought you meant literal rats," Mom explained.

I cursed, "How do we get rid of them?"

"Don't worry. They'll turn back eventually. Like a pumpkin carriage at midnight." Granny chuckled, amused by her own joke.

"Seems Maui will keep them busy until then," my mom commented as Maui zoomed past a table, knocking an antique lamp to the floor.

"What's going on with you anyway?" Granny asked. I waited until Maui had safely chased the rats up the staircase toward the attic before I climbed down from the counter. "You're really out of sorts tonight. I mean, I know you found a dead body this morning, but there's something else."

"I'm sorry. I'm just really nervous." I wiped my hands on the apron still tied around my neck. "Ugh. I forgot I'm still wearing this thing." I ripped the apron up over my head and stuffed it into a drawer.

"Why are you nervous? Is it that Harper?" Granny prodded.

I grimaced waiting for the inevitable lecture about keeping

my distance and witches not having romantic relationships with their Guardians.

"You don't have anything to be nervous about," she said instead. "He's the one who should be nervous. You're beautiful, smart, funny. And you're a freakin' witch. Need to work on your self-esteem a little, I suppose. But otherwise, you're a catch and any man would be lucky to have you. You need to know your worth, sweetheart."

"Thanks, Granny."

"Also, you need to learn to toot your own horn. 'Cause no one else is gonna toot it for you."

"Huh. That's actually really good advice."

"Of course it is! I'm very wise." She nodded in agreement with herself.

"Hey, Granny." I turned on the faucet to run cold water over the burn on my hand. "Can I ask you a question?"

"Anything." She adjusted her glasses.

"What happened to my grandfather?"

"Anything but that." She turned away and headed for the couch.

"Ma," my mother said in her disappointed tone.

"I've been here for a month now and have learned so much about our family, but not a single one of you nor anyone in our coven has mentioned him. I just... wondered what happened to him? At first, I thought maybe he died but he's not here and he's never visited, so... where is he?" I finished, giving Granny an expectant look. She paced the floor but refused to make eye contact.

"She doesn't like to talk about it," Mom said. "His name was Lucian Mandrake."

Granny pretended to spit.

"She's still bitter, I see." I said.

"That's probably an understatement." Mom said.

"Lucian Mandrake?" I asked, and Granny spit again. "That is a very sinister sounding name."

"If the shoe fits," Granny finally spoke.

"What's with all of the evil, villainous sounding names in this family, anyway? It's like we were named by a guy that writes fairy tales. Lucian Mandrake. Drusilla Rathmore."

"Hey, don't drag me into this. Besides, you're Drusilla Rathmore too." Granny wagged her finger at me.

"Sorry about that," Mom said sarcastically.

"She's lucky to have my name. And my genes. I mean, look what she has to look forward to." Granny held out her arms and struck a pose.

I smirked and decided to drop it for the time being. "What I have to look forward to is a circus. Which, coincidentally, I am *not* looking forward to."

"Oh, I am!" Granny clasped her hands together, no doubt happy about the change in conversation.

"You are?"

"Oh, yes. I love the circus. And I always say, there's too many freaks and not enough circuses."

"Granny, I don't think they still have freak shows at circuses."

"No? Well, that's too bad. I once saw a woman with four feet. Four! She braided her hair with two of them and threw knives at some dummy on a spinning board with the other two. Now *that* was entertainment!"

"Yes, I'm sure it was. So you're really going to go haunt the circus?"

"I'm not haunting. I just want to go have a little fun. I never get out anymore. I'm always stuck here with you and your obnoxious cat." That was true. Granny was a ghost, but the two of us were stuck together until I learned everything I needed to about my magic and fully came into my power. As far as my cat goes, she was right about that too.

"Besides," she continued, "someone has to keep an eye on you and Wolf Harper on your little date." She raised her eyebrows.

Ah, there it was. The lecture I'd been waiting for. "Granny, it's not a date. He's doing it for work. Anyway, Harper and I are just friends." Admittedly, I wouldn't have minded if we were more.

"That's what your mother used to say about your dad right up until the day he came and asked me for her hand in marriage."

"And you said yes?" I was shocked. My father had been my mother's Guardian just like Harper was mine.

"Well, you've met her. Do you really think it would've made a difference if I'd said no?" Granny said.

"Hey!" My mother pretended to be offended.

Granny turned to address her. "You know you were going to do what you wanted. Rules be damned."

"Couldn't you have used your magic to keep them apart?" I asked.

"The only thing stronger than magic is love. And now look at those two idiots. One is a raven and the other has been single for the last twenty-eight years. There's a reason we have these rules."

"Thanks, Ma," my mother said in a flat tone.

"So... it's not actually forbidden to be in a relationship with your guardian? Just a rule?" The wheels were turning in my head.

"An unwritten rule." Granny looked at me over the top of her glasses.

"So, basically just frowned upon," I said.

"It's a rule, Dru. I'm sure it's written down somewhere. It's not wise for a witch to get involved with her guardian. You know this. Your father is also wholeheartedly against the idea because of what happened to your mom. You need to find a nice human boy and go bother him."

I rolled my eyes. "I'm not going to bother anyone. And like I said, Harper and I are just friends." I was hoping if I said it enough times, I would start to believe it myself.

"Well, here comes your 'just friend.' That or you're the first victim in a campy horror movie, because there's a clown the size of a linebacker headed this way."

"Huh?" I glanced toward the front door just as it swung open. In strolled a clown donning a hideous bright yellow jump-suit, complete with traditional white face paint and a huge red wig. Doing a quick shuffle of his feet to show off his oversized shoes, he stuck his arms out wide and proclaimed, "Ta-da! What do you think?"

"Terrifying," I said.

"You don't like it?"

"Did you forget what I found waiting for me outside this morning?"

His face fell. "Wow." He pulled the wig from his head and ruffled a hand through his sandy blond hair. "I'm a jerk."

"Pretty insensitive," I teased.

"I'm sorry." He lowered his eyes.

"You should be. And now I have to look at your stupid clown face all night." I folded my arms across my chest.

He kept his head low but looking up at me and grinned. "I worked really hard on this, I'll have you know."

I laughed. "I'm sure you did. You look absurd. Why are you dressed as a clown though?"

Harper chuckled. "I take it you've sat down there in your bookstore for the last week with those flyers in front of you on the counter and didn't once take a look at one of them?" He pulled a folded-up piece of paper from his pocket and held it up, "See right here. Opening Night, adults only 9 p.m. to midnight. Come dressed as a clown for half off the price of admission." He slapped the flyer down on the kitchen counter. "The better question is why *aren't you* dressed as a clown? I was planning on paying for you, but not at full price."

"I am more than capable of paying for myself." I jutted my chin out.

"I'm just teasing you," Harper said, leaning on the counter. "There's no way I'm letting you pay for yourself." He honked his clown nose.

His sudden close proximity gave me nervous butterflies and I instinctively crossed my arms over my chest. "So, anything to report? Did you guys find any fingerprints or anything this morning?"

Harper shook his head. "No, ma'am. But hopefully we'll get something from the cigarette butt. It's at the lab as we speak."

"Not that murder isn't the priority, but what about the break-in? Nothing?"

"It appears to be a standard lock-pick. You really need a security system. I don't like that someone can just get in here that easily." He straightened and crossed his arms over his chest.

"I agree. But that's not really in the budget at the moment."

"It needs to be." He said firmly. "I'll take care of it."

"What do you mean?"

"I mean, I'll take care of it. Don't worry about it."

"Harper—" I started.

"Listen, I'm your Guardian, right? It's my job to keep you safe."

21

I wanted to ask him if there was more to it than that. That he wanted to keep me safe because he had feelings for me. Instead, I bit my tongue and gave him a polite smile.

"Thanks." I shoved a lock of hair behind my ear.

"It smells delicious in here by the way." He looked around. "What did you make?"

"Blueberry muffins." I motioned to the pile on the counter.

"No. I mean, those smell great too. But it's something else. Something...bacon?"

"Oh, well, I was planning on grocery shopping today but the dead clown kinda ruined my plans. So I ended up using what I had on hand and I made biscuits and gravy for dinner."

"But biscuits and gravy are a breakfast food." He knit his brow together.

"So?"

"So you ate it for dinner. You can't eat breakfast foods for dinner."

"You're joking, right?" I smirked.

"No. Why would I joke about something like that?" I studied his face for a moment and realized he was completely serious.

I laughed. "I'm almost thirty years old. I can eat breakfast foods anytime I please. You've really never had breakfast for dinner?"

He shook his head. "Just like I don't eat dinner foods for breakfast."

I rolled my eyes.

"I do love biscuits and gravy though. I suppose I'd be open to trying it for dinner sometime. You made bacon too?"

"Well, I made bacon gravy."

"Wait. What?"

"I made bacon gravy."

"Are you sure he doesn't have a hearing problem?" Granny mumbled from the couch and I was thankful he couldn't hear her.

"Wait. You're telling me you can make bacon gravy? That's a thing?" Harper continued.

"Yes, my grandma Davis used to make it all the time. So did my dad. You've never had it before?"

He shook his head.

"Well, you're in luck. I have a little leftover." I pulled the plastic bowl from the fridge and zapped it in the microwave. "You *have* to try this. It will change your world."

I held out a fork with a hearty portion of buttermilk biscuit drenched in bacon gravy. Harper lunged for it like a starving dog and I waited for his reaction.

"Oh. My. God." He sighed and his eyes rolled back in his head.

"Can I have it?" He motioned to the plastic bowl in my hand.

"Sure." I laughed.

"He acts like he hasn't eaten in days." Granny said.

"Dru, this is..." Harper stabbed his fork in the air and spoke with a mouthful of food. "This is like Christmas in my mouth."

"I told you it was good."

"Oh, it's better than that." He moaned and I felt a flutter in my stomach. Heat rushed to my cheeks and I decided to busy myself with wiping up the kitchen counters.

"Gross," Granny commented. I waved a dismissive hand in her direction and pretended to work on a stubborn spot on the countertop.

I felt the warmth of Harper's presence behind me and I turned to see him standing with the empty bowl in his hands. "Thanks." He grinned.

"You're welcome."

"You know, that rivals anything Peaches makes." Peaches, with her sweet southern drawl and soothing presence, was not only a witch too, but she also owned the little café in town and served up some of the best home cooking ever.

"And I'm not even a kitchen witch!" I shared my new knowledge.

Harper laughed as he rinsed the bowl and stacked it in the sink.

"You ready for what promises to be a magical night?" He asked.

I nodded.

Granny jumped from the couch and headed toward the front door. "Finally. Grab your purse and let's hit the road then."

"You're ridiculous." I laughed, "I just need to lock up."

"See ya there!" Granny threw her arm in the air as a goodbye.

"Oh, yeah, Granny's going too," I told Harper. I was the only one who could see or hear her, aside from other ghosts and animals, so I often had to act as a mediator. As such, a lot of what Granny *actually* said got conveniently lost in translation.

"Stay out of trouble, Granny!" Harper called out.

Even though he couldn't see her, she waved him off over her shoulder before disappearing through the door.

"Famous last words," I said sarcastically.

CHAPTER 3

"*W*ell, I think it's safe to say Granny was right. I've officially walked into my own horror movie." I grabbed onto Harper's bicep as we started into the circus and were met with an onslaught of flashing lights and distant music and other circus-goers dressed in clown costumes. The familiar smells of popcorn and caramel apples mingled together and wafted through the air; and I suddenly had a craving for a good old-fashioned elephant ear with a hefty sprinkling of cinnamon and sugar.

"You really don't like clowns, do you?" It was hard to tell through the face paint, but I was pretty sure he was giving me a sympathetic look.

"I really don't. Circuses either, if I'm being honest. I know they seem all fun and everything, but I feel like there's something dark and sinister about them. I've probably watched too many scary movies but they just creep me out." I gave an involuntary shudder. "Besides, there's most likely a murderer here tonight."

Harper wrapped his arm around me as we brushed past a

group of loud, drunken patrons dressed in a mishmash of clown attire and badly applied makeup and I felt that annoying fluttering in my stomach again.

"Dru!" I heard someone call my name and turned to see a few of my coven members trailing not far behind us. Sisters, Dorothy and Minnie, led the pack. They had been Granny's friends since childhood and I often wondered if there was ever a time when they hadn't bickered constantly. Minnie raised her arm in a theatrical wave, as if I wouldn't possibly see them without it, and Dorothy slapped at her hand and scowled in typical Dorothy fashion.

Tilly slipped past them and got to me first, wrapping me up in a quick embrace. She was in her early sixties and always a bit disheveled. Her short, vibrant red hair never quite managing to stay in place and, after knowing her for a short time, I was starting to believe that she wasn't one of those women that didn't know. Rather, she had just decided at some point that she didn't care.

"I didn't know you were coming tonight!" She'd been in the States longer than I'd been alive, but somehow she'd managed to preserve her British accent.

"I didn't either," I muttered.

Peaches, as we called her, bumped Tilly out of the way with a sassy hip move and threw her arms around me. Peaches owned the bustling café in town and was the quintessential southern woman. She wore a pink button up blouse that hugged her curvy figure and I noticed a button struggling to keep her large bosom from busting out to say hello.

"Hi, darlin'." She said and pulled me in for a strong hug, her pink and red bracelets jangling on her wrists. Peaches always gave the best hugs. The kind that made you feel warm and safe and like everything was right with the world. That and she always smelled like freshly baked cookies.

She pulled back and held me at arms' length. "Well, don't you just look pretty as a peach." Her bright blue eyes sparkled.

"Thanks, Peaches."

"And look at you!" She turned to Harper, flashing him a bright white smile. "You look like you're fixin' to leave us and join the circus yourself."

"No, ma'am." Harper gave a small laugh. "There's nowhere else I'd rather be than right down the street from the place that serves the best home cooking in the world." He winked.

Peaches blushed and gave his arm a playful slap.

"That is quite the getup," Dorothy said to Harper. She was taller than her sister, Minnie, clocking in at just under six feet, and she wore her gray hair in a short, well-styled cut. I was used to seeing her in pantsuits and matching jewelry, but tonight I noticed she'd traded in the kitten heels for sneakers.

"Oh, I like it!" Minnie beamed, her eyes sparkling, as she gave Harper a good once-over. Minnie was shorter and a bit rounder than her sister, but they always dressed in a similar fashion. Tonight, however, she wore a pink one-piece costume and had painted her face up like a happy clown. She was actually kind of adorable and I chuckled at the thought of how much Dorothy must've been hating it.

"Hello, ladies." A male voice came from behind them and I saw Eve and her husband, Pete, approaching. "And, sir," he added once he noticed Harper.

I had never met a couple who embodied the opposites attract cliché more than Eve and Pete. While she was free-spirited and well, a witch, Pete was type-A, practical—an accountant, for crying out loud. Eve's hair was a long mess of caramel-colored natural waves and she adorned herself with turquoise and coral jewelry and flowy clothing made of hemp. Pete wore an expensive watch, practical shoes, and even wore his T-shirts tucked in. Somehow though, they worked. They balanced each other out, and seeing them together always gave me hope.

"How are you doing, dear? Did you get a new lock on the door that was broken into?" Dorothy asked me.

"Yes, I'm fine. We replaced the doorknob too. Thanks again for taking care of that," I said to Pete.

"No problem. Happy to help." He smiled and I caught Eve giving him an adoring look.

"Do you think the murder that took place there and the store being broken into are related?" Dorothy addressed Harper.

"I don't think he's supposed to talk to us about it," Tilly interjected.

"I don't think I much care what he's supposed to do. I want to know that Dru is safe," Dorothy replied, never taking her eyes off of Harper. Dorothy was one of those tough as nails types, but once she let you past that exterior, she really had a heart of gold. I wondered if it was too late to see if she could be my Guardian. That might make my life a lot simpler. In more ways than one.

"Now, don't be ugly, Dorothy." Peaches warned in her sweet southern drawl, placing her hands on her hips.

"Dru is safe," Harper said curtly, but then his voice softened. "You know I'd never let anything happen to her."

Dorothy nodded, but turned to me. "Perhaps you should come stay with us. Just until the police figure this out."

"Oh! Yes! A slumber party!" Minnie bounced up onto her tiptoes and clapped her hands together.

"Oh, no, I'm fine. I couldn't impose." I started.

"It's not an imposition," Dorothy said.

"Don't be a bully, Dorothy. If she says she fine, then she is."

Peaches gave me an encouraging nod. Believe it or not, she was one of the younger members of our coven, about my mother's age, but she never had any trouble telling the older ladies what was what.

"Dorothy, really. I'm perfectly safe. Besides, I have Mom and Maui and Granny."

"And me." Harper cut in.

"And Harper. If I ever feel scared, I'll give you a call. Deal?"

*A*ll right." She nodded, seemingly satisfied. "Just know that we love you, and you're welcome to come stay with us anytime." She gave me a quick hug and I noticed her sneaking a glance at Harper as she pulled away. "We'll let you two have your evening. Come on, girls. And Pete."

We said our quick goodbyes and it was just Harper and I again.

"You know your safety is my number one priority, right?" He asked, and I realized Dorothy's comments must've genuinely bothered him.

"Sure. I mean, it's your job, right?"

"It is, but…" his voice trailed off. My stomach felt like it was in my throat and I noticed I was holding my breath.

"What should we do first?" He pointed to a sign. "It looks like the main event starts in thirty minutes and we want to get a good seat. Maybe we should just head that way now." He scanned the circus grounds eagerly and I couldn't help but feel a pang of disappointment at his sudden change in topic. Guess he wasn't going to profess his love for me after all. Even though he didn't know what I was thinking, I still felt a wave of embarrassment that I'd even thought it was a possibility.

"Oh wait. I know," Harper gave me a little squeeze, "How about a psychic reading? To get us warmed up?" He motioned to a tent with his free hand. Psychic readings by Madame Coralee, ten dollars."

"Wait, if a psychic works here, couldn't she just tell us who killed Chuckles the clown?" I asked.

"Why don't we go ask her?" He winked.

I groaned in response.

"Come on. It'll be fun." Harper pulled me toward the blue tent and I realized he was having way too much fun at my expense. Out of the corner of my eye, I caught a glimpse of a dark figure darting through the crowd. He wore an old fashioned top hat and long black coattail suit. He moved with urgency and I realized he had zeroed in on me.

I was about to say something to Harper as we reached the opening of the psychic's tent, when a man burst through the tent flaps, startling us both. It took me a moment to recognize him but it was Marvin the Magnificent.

"Marvin!" A woman followed close behind him. Given that she was dressed up like every stereotype of a psychic you could imagine, I assumed this must be Madame Coralee. She grabbed Marvin by the arm, her jewelry jangling loudly with her every move, and he spun around to face her.

"How dare you!" He spat, oblivious to the fact that Harper and I were witness to his tantrum.

"Marvin, please!" Coralee cried, her frizzy brown hair blown back by a light evening breeze.

"You will never speak of this again. Do you understand me?" Marvin's cheeks grew a deep shade of red and he ripped his arm from her grasp.

"Is everything all right?" Harper raised his voice and gave it an intentional edge, trying to assert his authority.

Marvin turned abruptly and smoothed a hand over the top of his bald head, taming the few strands of hair that had moved out of place.

"He probably doesn't recognize you in... that." I waved my hand in a circle over Harper's face.

"Oh, right." Harper pulled his badge from another hidden pocket. "Sergeant Harper. We met this morning."

"Oh, yes of course. Hello there, Sergeant. Nice to see you!" He held out his hand to Harper. "I'm so happy you've come to see our little circus!" He beamed as if he hadn't just been yelling at the poor woman wiping tears from her eyes behind him.

"Well, what can I say? We love the circus." Harper bumped my shoulder with his.

"Oh, wait, you're the poor dear who found Chuckles, aren't you? I recognize you from this morning." Marvin gave me a sympathetic look, "Coralee, this is the woman who found our Chuckles." He acknowledged me and reached out a kind hand to Coralee.

She took it as she stepped forward. In the light, I could see that she wasn't much older than me, though fine lines had already formed around her eyes and mouth, and her skin had taken on a leathery texture from too much time in the sun. She had heavy green makeup on her eyes and wore a deep purple lipstick that matched the scarf tied around her head. She held out a hand weighed down by countless rings and bracelets and they rattled and clinked with her every move.

"I'm Coralee. I'm so sorry you had to experience that. It must've just been terrible for you." She took my hand between both of hers and gave me a kind smile.

"Ah, thank you. And I'm sorry for your loss." I looked from her to Marvin.

"Yes, well, I'm confident you'll catch whoever did this," Marvin addressed Harper.

"I will." Harper clenched his jaw and I knew the wheels were turning in his head. I wished I had the power to read minds for about a half a second before I realized that ability might be more trouble than it was worth.

"Well, I have a show to prepare for. Will you two be coming to watch? We have some of the finest performers in the world, you know." Marvin nodded in agreement with himself.

"We will. But first, I think my friend here wanted to get a reading." Harper looked at me expectantly.

"Oh, but if you aren't up to it—" I started.

"Nonsense." Coralee cut me off and did a final quick swipe under each eye. "Come in. Come in." She motioned for us to follow her into her tent.

Marvin bowed his head before hurrying off, glancing at us over his shoulder as he went.

The inside of Coralee's tent was smaller than it appeared from the outside and lit with dozens of cheap string lights shaped like stars.

"Please sit." Coralee motioned to a chair across the table from her, spreading her hands across the deep purple tablecloth and smoothing its wrinkles.

I slid the rickety brown wicker chair across the dirt floor and positioned myself on it carefully, certain that it would give at any moment.

She had a deck of cards that she was shuffling back and forth between her hands. I noticed they were weathered, much like her face. I imagined her spending her days worshipping the sun, a free spirit reenergizing her soul through the moments she felt most at one with nature. Her dress was what one might describe as eccentric. An outfit of seemingly random patterns and colors, bracelets stacked halfway up her forearms and a ring for each finger.

"Can I see your hands?" She placed the cards on the table between us and rested her hands, palms up. I placed my hands in the warmth of hers and stole a quick glance at Harper. He was obviously amused.

Coralee closed her eyes and let out a small breath. The tent was small and barren, and I could hear nothing but the muffled sounds of circus patrons coming from outside the tent. As I tried to figure out where the smell of patchouli was coming from and realized it must've been Coralee herself, she ripped her hands out from under mine and her eyes popped open. They were as wide as silver dollars and clearly filled with distress.

She leaned across the table, so close I could feel her hot breath on my face.

"You're in danger."

Her huge dark eyes searched mine, and I felt Harper move close enough that I could feel the heat of his body next to me.

Coralee looked up at Harper. "You need to protect her. She's in imminent danger."

"All right." He gently touched my upper arm, indicating it was time for us to go.

"No. Listen to me." She stood, her hands gripping the table-cloth so tightly that her knuckles were snow white save the ripples of bluish veins that trailed through them.

"I'm curious. If you're a psychic, how come you didn't know Chuckles was in danger?" Harper asked in an accusatory tone.

"I did!" She raised her voice. "I tried to warn everyone, but no one ever believes me. They think I'm a fraud. Even my own troupe!" As she spoke, her eyes grew wild.

Harper grabbed me lightly under the arm and pulled me up from the chair that I'd found myself frozen in.

"Please, calm down, ma'am." He took a step in front of me and positioned himself between us. "Tell me what you... know."

She loosened her grip on the tablecloth and softened her hard expression. "You believe me?"

Harper nodded and I knew he was just placating her.

"I just get feelings about things sometimes. I had this terrible dread come over me and it lingered for days. Then I just woke up this morning and I knew something bad had happened to Chuckles. I told Marvin, but he didn't believe me. And everyone else just laughed it off." She put her face in her hands and shook her head. "But now he's dead!"

"But you didn't see or hear anything that led you to believe someone wanted him dead? It was just... feelings?" Harper asked.

She raised her head and narrowed her eyes at him. "I thought you believed me?"

"I do." He held up his hands defensively. "I'm just making sure there's not more to it. That you're not protecting someone, maybe?"

"I'm not," she said with a scowl.

"Okay. Thank you for your time." Harper put his arm around my shoulders and led me out of the tent.

Once we were safely outside, he leaned down close to my ear and whispered, "Circus folk."

CHAPTER 4

"*A*re you ready for this?" Harper asked, his eyes lit up excitedly.

"For what?" I balanced what was left of my elephant ear on a flimsy piece of butcher paper on my lap and sipped my soda through the straw.

"The Main Event! The big show!" He gestured to the patchy grass stage area in front of us. There was a small box near the front with the words "Braun Bros. Circus" and a setup for what I assumed was an acrobatic show.

I giggled and couldn't resist teasing him. "We're here because you love the circus, aren't we? The whole 'undercover investigation' thing is a ruse, isn't it?"

He pretended to look hurt. "How dare you question my professionalism."

I plucked the last bite of elephant ear from my lap and crinkled the paper up into a ball. "Harper," I leaned in close enough to smell his aftershave and lowered my voice barely above a whisper, "first of all, you're a shapeshifter. It would be much easier to do undercover work as literally anything other than a

6'2" clown. And second, and I can't stress this enough, you're dressed like a clown." Harper was my Guardian, but he was also a shapeshifter. He wasn't restricted to one animal though. He was able to shift into anything he wanted to, even another person.

"Uh, that's the undercover part. No one at the precinct but Chief Carver knows I'm a... you know." He made a show of glancing around to demonstrate how important it was that no one was listening to our conversation.

"That is... such a weak argument."

"Fine. Yes, I love the circus. Who doesn't?" He snatched my soda from my hand and took a drink.

"We're sharing drinks now?" I teased.

"You owe me." He handed it back.

"I owe you? For paying?"

"No, for trying to kill me." He winked.

I groaned. "You're never going to let me live that down, are you?"

"Never." He leaned in and playfully bumped my shoulder with his.

The lights dimmed across the seating area and Harper's eyes widened in excitement. "It's starting!" he whispered.

I chuckled to myself at his childlike enthusiasm and turned my attention to the stage. A woman began to slowly walk toward the small podium and I instantly recognized her. It was Elsa, the woman who had been at my building that morning with Marvin the Magnificent. She had her blonde hair pinned up, her lips painted a bold red color, and perfect, rosy cheeks. A black fur boa was draped elegantly around her arms, and she wore a form-fitting red dress and matching heels. She stepped carefully onto the podium, her head held high, and I could tell she'd done it a million times before. Marvin came forward carrying an old-fashioned microphone stand in his hands that he set in front of Elsa. Pulling the microphone from its stand, he waved his free hand as he spoke.

"Welcome, welcome, ladies and gentlemen!" He paused, waiting for the crowd to quiet down. Once he was satisfied that he had everyone's attention, he continued, moving back and forth theatrically.

"Tonight, you will see daring stunts, fantastical feats, and death-defying performances. We have the best performers in the world, after all. Our acrobats are world-renowned, our sword-swallowing, fire-eating woman will have you in awe, our clowns will have you in fits of laughter, and our magician will boggle your mind." He paused for effect. "And now, before we start the show, a very special welcome to you all from the beautiful Elsa Braun! I can assure you—you have never heard a voice this angelic before. Welcome, all, to the Braun Brothers Circus!"

The crowd erupted in a thunderous applause and he placed the microphone back on its stand. Elsa stared out into the crowd while he moved it as close to the podium as possible. She took a small step forward as a soft melody came from speakers hidden somewhere. A hush fell over the crowd as she opened her mouth and began to sing. Harper and I both turned to each other, mouths hanging open.

"She's amazing," I whispered. Her voice had a sort of sadness to it that didn't quite match the peppy circus vibe, but she belted out the words nevertheless. In fact, she may've had the most beautiful voice I ever heard.

I scanned the stage area around her. It was dark, but I could see the shadows of other circus performers, mostly clowns, a few of them whispering to each other. I somehow caught the eye of a man standing alone, leaning nonchalantly against a stack of platforms, and I realized it was the man in the top hat from earlier that I'd spotted when we first arrived. He was hard to see in the shadows, but I could feel his eyes boring into me. Why was he fixated on me, of all people? I shrunk down in my seat and scooted closer to Harper until my shoulder was touching his.

The man turned his attention from me and disappeared farther into the darkness behind him. I shuddered a little and Harper put his arm around me.

"Cold?" He asked.

"I'm okay," I lied. Something about the man gave me a bad feeling, and it wasn't just his weird, old-timey outfit.

Elsa finished her song, her lovely voice booming through the tent. Everyone jumped to their feet in applause and her face absolutely radiated delight. She smiled and gave a small bow before stepping from the podium and gliding away.

"Beautiful, Elsa! Just beautiful!" Marvin praised her before addressing the crowd. "Have you ever heard such a heavenly voice? So lovely." He waited for the cheering to die down before he raised the microphone to his lips again.

"Up next, we have a wonderful show for you. Bold and death-defying feats will be performed by some of the most cele-brated acrobats in the world! But first, I want to introduce you to a very special man. A man who is so mysterious—so enig-matic—he may not even really be a man at all." He paused and looked from one side of the tent to the other. "Please give a round of applause for Ridley, the greatest magician in the world!"

The crowd clapped as the mystery man from before walked to the center of the arena. He stopped next to the podium and stood stiffly, an uninterested expression on his face. He waited until the applause had completely died down and the only noise in the tent was the intermittent cough or murmur.

Satisfied, he pulled something small from his coat pocket and brought it to his mouth. He began to play a soft melody and I realized it was a harmonica. There was something both beautiful and haunting about the tune he played and it sent a shiver down my spine for the umpteenth time that day. I watched him play, fascinated and slightly mesmerized, but also confused about why a magician was playing music.

"Don't listen, Dru," I heard Granny unexpectedly next to me.

I turned to face her, sitting in the empty seat on my right, but was immediately drawn back to the magician.

"Why?" I managed to whisper.

"Don't!" she said more urgently.

"How though?" I found myself unable to turn away from him this time.

"Stuff your hair in your ears," she said sarcastically. "Just don't use your magic. It's too unpredictable right now. Instead, focus on it, sing a song over and over again in your head, and block out the sound of the tune he's playing."

I did as instructed, closing my eyes and feeling my magic concentrated in the center of my chest, and desperately tried to think of a song I knew all the words to. I decided to play it safe and go with the ABCs. I was pretty confident I couldn't mess up the words to that one.

I forced myself to concentrate on the song like I was learning it for the first time, and somewhere around the sixth round, I realized that the music had finally stopped. Opening my eyes, I saw him still standing in the same spot. He kept his eyes on the crowd as he carefully slid the instrument back into his pocket. It dawned on me that no one was clapping, which seemed odd given how rowdy the crowd had been earlier. Perhaps he was waiting for some applause? He certainly deserved it, even though the music was an odd act for a magician. I was still confused about what was happening, but I set my soda on the ground between my feet and started to bring my hands together when Granny spoke again.

"Don't move, Dru," she said sternly.

I froze, hands still poised in front of me.

"Just wait."

I watched the magician scan the crowd one final, agonizingly slow time, hunkering down as low as I could next to Harper. When he seemed pleased, he took a gleeful little hop up onto the podium and sat at its edge. He pulled what appeared to be a small pocket knife from his pocket and a shiny green apple.

"Very, very carefully look at the people around you," Granny said. "Don't let him see you."

I darted my eyes around at the people seated in front of me. I could only see the backs of their heads, but they seemed frozen in place. I peered out at the stage area in front of me, trying to see the other circus performers who'd been hiding in the darkness. They were hard to make out, shadowy figures at best, but they too, were motionless. The magician set to work using the pocket knife to cut small sections from the apple and I took the opportunity to sneak a sideways glance at Harper. He sat rigidly on the edge of his seat, a huge smile stuck on his face, but his eyes were completely glazed over. I looked past him at the row of people seated next to him. They all had the same strange look.

"He's got bard magic," Granny finally said.

I straightened back in my seat and watched him continue to slice strips from his apple.

"A what?" I whispered.

"A *bard*," she hissed, as if I only hadn't heard her the first time instead of the fact that I had no idea what a bard was.

The magician stood, carefully placing his pocket knife back into his pocket and trading it out for the harmonica. He brought the instrument to his lips again and this time he played a quick, upbeat tune. It last only seconds but when he finished, he hurriedly shoved the instrument back in his pocket before spreading his arms out wide. Suddenly, Harper burst from his seat next to me, clapping his hands wildly. The entire tent erupted into loud cheers and I caught a smug smile form on the magician's face right before his grandiose bow.

After a painfully long round of applause, Harper sat down and gave me a pleased look. "Oh, man. That was great, wasn't it?"

I sat speechless for a moment, unable to figure out how to explain what had just happened, before Marvin's voice came over the microphone struggling to be heard above the cheering crowd.

"Granny?" I whispered, frantically scanning the tent for her, but she was gone. Marvin was saying something about acrobats, and when I looked back to the center of the tent, a small car came roaring out from somewhere in the darkness. It pulled to an abrupt stop and the door flew open, a sea of vibrantly-colored bodies came piling out, all falling on top of each other for comedic effect. *Yay. Clowns.* There had to have been at least eight clowns from the car and running behind the car was another clown, though this one was dressed as a police officer. He chased them around the arena and cringy slapstick comedy ensued. I heard Harper laughing beside me.

I narrowed my eyes, trying to see if the magician was still in the tent, but I didn't spot him anywhere. Harper was saying something about how great the performance was and I turned my attention back to the clowns just in time to watch the police officer clown chase the rest of them toward the ladder leading up to one platform. He pretended to fall so they could make their escape. They made a line on the ladder up to the platform, each pretending they were either scared or about to fall.

The first clown made it to the platform and I noted his odd outfit choice. It was light blue and spandex with three white puffball buttons down the front. His face paint seemed more in line with a mime than a clown, and I got the distinct impression that he was trying to stand out in some way.

He grabbed onto the first bar and swung out, doing flips in the air and landing on the second bar by the backs of his knees.

Okay, *that* was at least impressive.

The crowd gasped and I couldn't help but clap right along with them. He swung back and forth, picking up speed, and I was certain the entire tent was anticipating his next stunt. I spotted the cop clown out of the corner of my eye, climbing the ladder and shaking his fist. I rolled my eyes, but Harper was eating it up.

The spandex-suited clown swung higher and higher, until he finally flew through the air, performing countless flips as he went. He grasped the third bar and the crowd gasped and rang out in cheers. Right before one side of the bar broke and he fell to his death.

CHAPTER 5

I've heard about stampeding crowds and pandemonium breaking out in small spaces, but experiencing that kind of chaos firsthand? That was new.

Fortunately, Harper wasn't the only member of law enforcement posing as a guest that night, but you would've thought he was the way he sprung into action. The handful of police officers, including Chief Carver, and some of the circus staging crew were able to herd the panicked masses out of the tent so they could secure the area and await additional emergency personnel.

Once outside, most of the previously delighted circus-goers moved in a sort of dazed state toward the exit. If it hadn't been for the tearful, shocked looks on so many faces, I would've likened them to zombies. I had managed to track down Granny, or rather, she found me, sort of loitering out of the way near the porta-potties.

"Thank goodness there are no kids here tonight. Can you imagine?" Granny said.

I shuddered. "I know. That would've been traumatizing."

"Yeah, it was really intense. Get it? *In tents*?"

I couldn't help but laugh at her dumb joke, even at a time like this. "Can you please explain to me what happened in there now?"

"You mean with the magician?"

"Yes!" I said louder than I intended. I looked around to make sure no one noticed the crazy lady talking to herself, but the circus grounds had cleared out pretty fast and those who remained were far too busy to pay much attention to little ol' me.

"I'm not entirely sure just yet," Granny said. "I haven't seen one for a very long time."

"But how does he have magic? I thought men couldn't be witches?"

"Who told you that?"

"Heather."

"Heather also tried to kill you, so maybe don't take everything she said as gospel."

"Ha. Good point. So men *can* be witches then?" I kept my gaze on the big top tent, hoping to catch a glimpse of Harper emerging.

"Yes. Well, no. It's complicated."

"Give me the quick and dirty version."

"They can't be witches in the way that we define it. They aren't born with magic like us. Like I told you before, regular people can tap into magic if they know what they're doing. They study, they practice, they learn from a mentor. Like an apprentice. They can also acquire it from witches."

"They can?" I said, unable to mask my surprise. "How?"

"It's typically presented as a gift. Except no witch is giving up her powers. Every other witch knows that, which is why she'd target some unsuspecting human. It also means that there's some kind of curse tied to it that she hasn't been able to break. That's the only reason she'd pass it off to a human. That wizard in there, I don't know how he got his magic, but he's pretty good. He was able to use it on our coven. And those ladies are a tough crowd. You were the only one in there unaffected."

"Great." I sighed. "How am I supposed to deal with a magical bard, wizard, whatever when *my* magic is all messed up right now?"

"Best to avoid him for now. And avoid using your magic. We don't want anyone finding out what you really are. But you *have* to find your ring."

I nodded. This was going to be tough. I mean, granted I really wasn't that great at using my magic anyway, but I'd spent the last month actively trying to use it and still had difficulty controlling it. Now I had to actively try *not* to use it, without the help of my ring, find said ring, avoid a magical man, and figure out who killed Chuckles before I woke up to the sound of ghostly laughter and a hideous, creepy clown staring down at me. I shuddered at the thought.

"Have you seen the girls?" Granny asked, referring to the members of our coven that we'd seen earlier that night.

I looked around, trying to remember what colors they had been wearing in the hopes it would be easier to spot them.

"Dru!" I heard my name and spotted them moving in the wrong direction through a small crowd of people. Just as they had almost reached me, a group of teenage boys pushed past them. The one on the outside bumped hard against Dorothy's shoulder.

"Hey, watch out, grandma!" He turned and yelled at her.

Dorothy brought her hand to her chest and took a step back and Peaches gasped.

"Hey, come on, man," one of his friends said, motioning for him to keep moving.

"Dude, she made me spill my drink. Stupid old cow," he said angrily.

"Why, I got a mind to—" Peaches put one hand on her hip and used her other to jab her finger in the boy's direction, "Who's your mama, boy? Does she know you speak to your elders that way?"

Dorothy grabbed Peaches by the wrist and pulled her along. They continued to move toward me, in unison with everyone else, but I watched her smirk and give a subtle flick of her finger. Something like a volcanic explosion of soda happened behind her and I heard shouting and cursing. Over her shoulder, I could see the boy who'd been so rude, drenched and standing there motionless like he wasn't sure what to do. It was a little hard to hear over Granny's laughter, but it sounded like confused chatter coming from his friends just as my coven approached.

"That ought to teach him." I smiled at Dorothy.

"Not likely. But it felt good." She winked.

"Were you at the show, Dru? Did you see what happened?" Minnie asked.

I nodded. "Yeah. There's something I need to tell you guys though." I looked around. Most everyone had cleared out, just a few stragglers remained, standing in close huddles and speaking in hushed tones. "The magician in there. Granny said he's a wizard. A bard."

Minnie and Tilly both gasped.

'Heavens to Betsy!" Peaches widened her eyes in surprise.

"How does she know?" Dorothy scrunched up her brow.

"He played a song in there and everyone was just... I don't know. Frozen in place or something. It was so strange. And then he played something else and the crowd came back, so to speak."

"Even us?" Minnie asked.

"Yes, even us, Minnie." Dorothy had her arms crossed over her chest and gave her sister a side-long glance.

"What did you all see anyway?"

They all glanced at each other.

"I don't really remember," Tilly finally spoke up. "I remember he pulled out a harmonica, right?"

"Yes, the rest feels foggy. Until the end," Dorothy said.

Peaches and Minnie nodded in agreement.

"Yes, I just remember having this feeling that it was an amazing magic show. But that part of the night is quite foggy, as Dorothy said." Tilly shook her head.

"Did she explain to you what a bard is then?" Dorothy asked.

"She did. Uh, mostly," I answered.

"What do you mean *mostly*?" Granny asked.

"What did she suggest we do?" Dorothy asked me, but she glanced at Tilly and Peaches.

"Nothing yet. She just told me to stay away from him and not to use my magic."

Normally, Minnie has a confused look on her face, but when everyone else does as well, I know further explanation is required.

"I misplaced my ring."

Minnie gasped again and Dorothy widened her eyes.

"I'll find it!" I said, feeling like a broken record.

"Oh, dear." Minnie was wringing her hands together.

"We should high tail it out of here then," Peaches said.

Dorothy nodded. "His magic worked on us. Granted we

didn't know to watch out for it, but I'm really not in the mood to play with fire tonight."

"How are you getting home?" Tilly asked me.

"I'm waiting for Harper," I explained.

"I'm sure he'll be here all night, dear. Why don't you go with us?"

"Oh, no, that's okay. You all go on home. I know Harper will be busy tonight, but I just want to say goodbye before I go."

"Should we wait with you?" Minnie asked.

"Maybe we should. Since there's another possible threat we need to be careful about," Dorothy said.

I shook my head. "No, I'm fine. Really. Granny is here with me. I'll be fine. Promise." I smiled, trying my best to reassure them.

They all looked at each other, no doubt trying to decide what to do.

"Go. Really," I urged.

I received begrudging hugs before they left, and I caught them each looking back at me a few times as they headed for the exit.

"What *are* we still doing here, anyway?" Granny asked, pulling her long knit cardigan tight around her.

"I don't know. I'm kind of waiting for Harper, I guess. When everything happened, he told me to stay close. And then when everyone was taken outside, I kind of motioned to him that I'd be waiting out here."

"Why does he want you to hang around?"

"I'm not sure. I just have a feeling I shouldn't leave yet."

"Did you see the acrobat's ghost?"

"No, but I can't imagine he survived that fall."

Granny chuckled.

"What's so funny?"

"He's stuck as a clown now for all eternity."

"What do you mean?"

"Whatever you're wearing when you die. That's your ghost uniform."

I cringed. So if the ghosts of Chuckles and the newly expired clown *did* show up, then I had two ghost clowns to contend with. Fantastic.

"Moral of the story: try not to die while you're in your underwear. Or worse, naked. Especially if you've got the body of a hairy potato."

"Gross!" I smiled but was slightly distracted by the large clown that was finally headed my way.

"Hey, you doing okay?" Harper stopped in front of me and rested his hands on his hips.

I nodded. "Yeah, it's just kind of chaotic. And that was... shocking."

"Yeah, I'm sorry. Not what I envisioned for us this evening," he said, and I wondered what exactly he did envision.

"Dru," Granny said in a warning tone. If I didn't know better, I would've sworn she could read my mind sometimes.

"So what are you thinking?" I ignored her and directed my comment at Harper.

"What do you mean?"

"With two victims from the same circus now, what are the chances that was really an accident?" I lowered my voice.

He nodded. "Exactly what I was thinking." He looked around for a moment before he spoke. "Dobson just told me that they discovered that the wad of paper that was stuffed into Chuckles' mouth was one of the circus flyers."

"Yikes." I cringed.

"Yeah, there's something going on with this circus troupe

and for some reason it's all come to a head right here in Black-wood Bay."

"By the way, that magician, Granny said he's a bard," I said.

Harper knitted his brow together.

"I don't really know what that means either, but apparently he uses music to control his magic. You know when he brought out that harmonica?"

Harper's eyes darted around like he was trying to remember but was having trouble doing so. "Kind of," he finally said.

"You were in like some weird trance. Everyone was. And then there was no magic show. He just... he ate an apple."

"An apple?" Harper raised his eyebrows.

"Yeah, like he sat down and had a... a snack. It was weird. Anyway, then he played another song and brought you all ... I don't know... back," I tried to explain.

Harper looked around for a moment. "Okay, I need to get back inside. See if we can examine the equipment more closely and figure out what happened in there. Is Granny with you?"

"Why?"

"It's best if you head home now. And you should probably go while the rest of the crowd is still trickling out. Granny can be your fearless escort."

I started to protest but thought better of it.

He read the disappoint in my eyes. "Dru, I probably will need your help. The circus crew might think they're one big happy family but I bet the two men that are dead don't. They may be more willing to talk. We also need to figure out this bard business. But tomorrow. When the situation has de-escalated and it's daylight and I can keep a closer eye on you. For now, home."

"Fine."

"You have your cell phone?"

I nodded.

"Just let me know the second you get home, all right?"

"Yes, sir." I saluted Harper and caught an eye roll before I brushed past him.

I waited until Harper was out of earshot before I spoke. "Okay, I think we should probably split up. Cover more ground that way," I said to Granny before I realized she wasn't at my side. I turned and caught her headed toward the circus exit.

I took a quick look around and didn't see any people within earshot. "Granny! Wait. You can't just leave. I need your help."

She stopped and gave me a slow, dramatic turn before she spoke. "Oh? I thought we were leaving."

"Why would you think that?"

She crossed her arms over her chest.

"Granny, I can't go home. Ghost clowns, remember? I'll just be up all night. I might as well poke around here a little and see if I can find anything."

"Harper isn't going to like that, you know." She raised an eyebrow.

"Since when do you care about the permission of men?"

She set her jaw. *Bingo.* I knew I'd hooked her.

"Fine. I'll stay. But I'm going to complain the entire time."

"I wouldn't expect any less," I teased. "I'm going to go check around the big top tent. Hopefully the acrobat is there. Do you want to see if you can find Chuckles? Maybe he's wandering around here somewhere."

"If I must." She heaved an overly dramatic sigh. "Watch out for the bard. If you see him, avoid him at all costs. We don't know what else he's capable of yet." She turned and headed farther into the darkness of the night, away from the bright lights surrounding the main path. "Holler if you need me," she called over her shoulder.

I considered my options for a moment. I did *not* want to see any dead clowns, but if I had to, now might be the best time. The tent where the acrobat had died was still crawling with police and Harper was nearby in case something happened. He might be mad I'd stayed, but I'd rather deal with him than scary ghosts.

I headed back toward the red-and-white-striped tent but veered away from the entrance and made my way toward the back. The lighting was dim, only bright enough to see a few steps in front of me, so I slid my cell phone from the back pocket of my jeans and flipped on the flashlight. I heard voices coming from inside the tent and peeked through a small opening.

"Yeah, you see..." A tall man still dressed in clown garb was speaking. He pointed up to the offending trapeze bar. It was dangling from one side, and still swinging ever so slightly. "The mechanism there has been tampered with," he was saying.

"I can't say I'm surprised." Harper was standing next to him.

"Who do you think would do this, Officer?" he asked. "Sorry, I'm Jimmy." He held out his hand and introduced himself.

"Well, Jimmy, after what happened to Chuckles sometime last night, I think the odds are pretty good that it was someone from your circus troupe."

"It wasn't none of us." I heard another man's voice and noticed a little person who I instantly recognized as the policeman clown. I mean, he was still dressed in his costume, though he'd removed his hat, so it wasn't that hard to recognize him.

"And you are?" Harper asked.

"I'm Lucky," he introduced himself but kept his hands

stuffed deep in his pockets. "Listen. I been with this circus a long time. *Most* of us have been here a long, long time."

"Are you lost?" A deep, velvety voice came from the darkness somewhere nearby and I jumped. I felt the hair raise on my arms as I lifted the flashlight of my phone toward him. The bard struck a casual pose, leaning against a dirty trailer, one leg bent at the knee and his foot resting flat against the side of the trailer. His top hat was still on his head, but he'd unbuttoned his suit jacket, revealing a loosely tucked white dress shirt.

"Uh… I was just…" I stumbled over my words, struggling to come up with something to say.

"Spying? Snooping? What term would you prefer? You're not supposed to be back here anyway," he said flatly.

"Are you with the circus then?" I asked, feigning stupidity.

"Is that a rhetorical question?"

"You're not dressed like a clown."

"Brilliant observation," he deadpanned.

"Wow. I bet you're fun at parties," I quipped. "Marvin said the crew dressed like clowns on opening night."

"Marvin's always dressed like a clown. He just doesn't usually know it." He smirked. An uncomfortable silence hung in the air between us and I searched my mind for something to fill it.

"I'm sorry about your friends," I finally managed.

"I don't have any friends." he replied, pushing off from the trailer with his foot and taking a step toward me. He studied me for a moment, his head cocked to the side. "Are you from around here?" He pulled a cigarette and book of matches from a pack in his coat pocket and took a long first drag, the end of the cigarette burning a bright orange in the dark night. I tried to catch a glimpse of the filtered end, but it was too dark.

I considered the question for a moment. I was going to lie

but thought it might be better if he thought I was known around here, that people would be looking for me.

He exhaled slowly before he asked, "What's your name?"

"My name?" My stomach was officially doing somersaults. I wanted to scan the area with my eyes, see if anyone was close enough to hear me if I yelled, but I was afraid to take my eyes off of him.

He didn't answer, just stared at me intently.

"Tiffany. Tiffany Goldwait," I lied. I mean, a month ago she'd said she was me when it was convenient for *her*. It was only fair I return the favor.

He narrowed his eyes at me. "Tiffany Goldwait," he repeated.

I nodded and wondered if I could magically will my taser from the drawer of my nightstand into my pocket, but then I remembered that I wasn't supposed to be doing any kind of magic at all.

"Interesting hair... Tiffany." He blew a puff of smoke from his mouth and gave me a half smile that read much more sinister than friendly.

"Yeah, thanks." I pulled at a strand of hair that had fallen over my shoulder and took a step backward.

"That was no accident in there, you know." A smile tugged at the corner of his mouth.

"You're not scaring the guests again, are you?" A familiar German accent radiated into the night and I felt a comforting sense of relief wash over me.

Elsa sauntered toward us, still looking like she'd just been done up for a film in spite of the horror that we'd all just witnessed.

"Part of being mysterious requires inciting a certain level of fear, don't you think?" He spoke into the darkness, not really directing his response at either of us.

"We've been summoned to convene near the big top entrance, Ridley," she said without looking at him.

"Come with me." Elsa motioned for me to come toward her. "You really shouldn't be back here. It's dark. And dangerous." She shot a look at the magician, but he just stared at the burning end of his cigarette.

We'd made it just a few feet away when I heard his voice behind me, sending another chill up my spine.

"You make your own mind up about what's lurking in the shadows. Sometimes, the villain hides in plain sight."

CHAPTER 6

"Thanks," I said to Elsa, quickening my pace to keep up with her.

She gave me a slight nod and a tight smile, but continued to look straight ahead.

"I'm sorry about what's happened to your friends," I offered.

She waved a dismissive hand. "I'm sorry my performers have decided to start killing each other—quite literally—in your little town." She let out a short burst of nervous laughter.

Not exactly the reaction I expected, but shock and grief can make people act a little strange.

"I heard you mention this morning that your father owned this circus?"

"Oh, yes." Her eyes lit up at the mention of him. "He was a knife thrower first. And when the previous owner died, my father took over. The only ringmaster circus clown. He prided himself on that. But I still keep his old throwing knives." Her eyes glazed over, and she suddenly seemed far away. "A reminder of simpler times, you know?"

Moving states away from my father and my home, discovering I was a witch, meeting my mother and grandmother, and working through feelings I had for a Guardian that I wasn't supposed to have feelings for? Yeah, I knew 'simpler times.'

"How long has he been gone?" I asked.

"Oh, five years now," she said, her voice wistful.

"I'm sorry for your loss." I paused. "How did Marvin end up being the one to take over?"

"Well, he came to us ten or so years ago and worked as my father's assistant. Papa was getting old and couldn't do as much. You know how that is. When he passed, it only made sense that I give the job to Marvin."

"I see."

"It was the right choice," she continued, "because the performers really took to him. Which is more than I can say for myself." She laughed nervously again.

"You don't get along with them?"

"Ha. Well," she said, looking down and watching her feet as she walked, "in this day and age, one would think having a woman in charge wouldn't be such a struggle for people. But, speaking from experience, it seems that when a man is calling the shots, he's strong," she held up her arms and pretended to flex, "and a great leader. He's admired. But when it's a woman, she's bossy and hysterical and well, quite frankly... a witch." She scoffed. "So I let Marvin take over when it came to dealing with the performers. It was just easier that way."

We reached the other side of the big top tent and I saw Harper standing in front of the circus troupe. It was the first time I'd really seen them all. There were the clowns I'd seen performing, the woman who'd been billed as a fire-eater and a sword swallower—an act I was actually disappointed that we'd missed, the strong man—at least I assumed that was his role given his monster appearance, and a dozen other performers and crew members who I didn't recognize. I looked around but didn't see Coralee anywhere. I had a sinking feeling that Harper would be mad that I'd stuck around when I wasn't supposed to. I'd been hoping to avoid him unless I found something useful, but as usual, things didn't go quite as planned. He caught me approaching with Elsa and shot me a sharp look.

Okay, yes, definitely mad.

He waited for us to join the group before he spoke, taking a moment too long to make sure I saw the disappointed look he was giving me.

"What's going on, sir?" Marvin finally spoke up impatiently.

"We've confirmed that the trapeze accident was no accident."

A few performers gasped and clutched each other.

"Why, that just can't be!" Marvin took his handkerchief from his pocket and dabbed at his forehead.

I heard a muffled sound and glanced in Elsa's direction. She remained stoic, a few single tears tracing their way down her slightly sunken cheeks. She wasn't making that ugly cry face— you know the one. Me? I hate crying in front of people because I make the most hideous faces. I'm always envious, and in awe, of people who can just have tears sliding down their perfect, beautiful faces. What kind of sorcery is that, anyway? Elsa caught me staring and used the back of her hand to dry her cheeks.

"What do you mean it wasn't an accident? I don't under-stand," she said.

"It appears the trapeze was tampered with. Someone wanted it to break once it had some weight on it." Harper paused and I knew he was studying the crowd for tells. "Did

Ferdinand always go first? Was that the typical routine?" His name was *Ferdinand*? His costume, which had hugged him in all the inappropriate places, had certainly been a clue, but the fact that he still went by Ferdinand only confirmed that he didn't embrace the whole clown experience like some of the other performers.

"Yes, he did." The sword-swallowing, fire-eating woman spoke up. Her hair was a navy blue color and kept in a short buzz cut. While she wore a simple tank top and combat boots, she did wear a painted clown face. The other performers, aside from the standard sad clown, went with the typical happy-go-lucky style of makeup. But she had opted for something a bit darker, with lots of black and blood red, and I was surprised Marvin had allowed something so frightening. I silently thanked the murderer for not having killed her and vowed to find him just in case she was next on his list.

Harper had pulled the wig from his head and was speaking to the group. "We'll be here through the night investigating. We'll be talking to each of you. Probably more than once. We ask that you all go to your trailers and keep them locked. Do not open the door for anyone other than myself or one of the policemen you recognize here tonight."

"You think there's a circus performer serial killer?" someone spoke up.

"I think someone wasn't happy with Chuckles and Ferdinand. And it's a strong possibility that they aren't happy with some more of you."

There was panicked murmuring and a lot of side-long, distrustful glances as the group dispersed.

"Alone!" Harper called out behind them. "Go to your trailers alone! An officer will be by to check in with you shortly."

The strong man filled the space between Harper and I and I took the opportunity to try to sneak past him.

"Dru," Harper said my name and I felt my stomach flip— but not in the good way.

Turning to face him, my mind worked a mile a minute as I tried to come up with what I was going to say.

He had his hands rested on his hips and he was grinding his teeth.

"Look, I'm guessing you're mad—" I started.

"I'm not *mad*," he interrupted. "I'm just disappointed."

Great. "Okay, Dad." I rolled my eyes. "I know you told me to go home, but let's think about this logically."

He crossed his arms over his chest and gave me a patronizing look.

"As you know, I found a dead clown on my property this morning. Now, let's forget the very creepy reality that he may show back up and stick with the facts. Is my place really the safest? Not only was my store broken into, but a literal murder occurred there last night. What if the murderer comes back because he thinks there may have been a witness? Another man was killed tonight so we know, whoever he is, this killer wasn't a one-hit wonder. And you're just going to send me off all alone? I mean, you're my Guardian, aren't you? Shouldn't I stay with you until we catch whoever did it?" I finished, feeling satisfied that I'd made a strong case.

I saw a look cross his face that I hadn't seen before. "Well, you aren't wrong." Harper thought for a moment before turning his head slightly and calling over his shoulder. "Dobson!"

He turned back to me, a half smile tugging at the corner of his mouth. "Dobson will get you home and stay with you until I can come check in. Probably won't be until sometime tomorrow."

"Wait. No, that's not going to work—" I started to protest, but Dobson was already on his way over and Harper turned to give him his orders.

"Now, you did it." Granny chuckled. I hadn't realized she'd approached, but she didn't stop, just slowed down as she passed. "Since you've got a bodyguard tonight, I'll be home late."

"What? Where are you going?" I hissed.

"I've got plans. See ya!" She called over her shoulder. *Plans? What kind of plans does an eighty-year-old ghost have?*

"Ready to hit the road?" Dobson asked eagerly. He was roughly my age, and a hulking ex-Marine who still sported a tight crewcut. People always seemed to give him a wide berth, but he was probably one of the gentlest people I'd ever met in my life. Picture an animated princess saving the innocent and then breaking into song with the cute little woodland creatures. Just replace the princess with one of those guys who looked like he could rip a tree stump from the ground with his bare hands and boom: that's Dobson.

"Yup, let's go." I looped my arm through Dobson's and cast my most sober, unbothered look at Harper. I know—I was being a total brat, even though he was only trying to look out for me. But I felt safest staying wherever he was. I just couldn't say that to him.

He was my Guardian, so of course I was supposed to feel safe with him. But this was something else. A feeling that felt so familiar but that I couldn't quite place.

"Did you see it?" Dobson interrupted my thoughts.

"See what?"

"That fall. Man, that was brutal."

"Oh, yeah," I said absentmindedly, feeling guilty about the way I'd given Harper an attitude.

We were drawing closer to the exit and I glanced over at Coralee's tent. Her sign had fallen to the ground, no doubt during the commotion from earlier.

"Hang on," I said to Dobson. Leaning over, I picked it up, dusting the dirt from its front and went to hang it back onto the metal hook. That's when I heard the light sobs. I hesitated a moment. I'd never been very good at dealing with other people's emotions. I always felt like I said the wrong thing. But it wasn't like me to leave someone to cry alone.

"Uh... Coralee?" I said.

"What are you doing?" Dobson stepped toward me.

I held up a hand to him, "Just a minute."

The tent flap drew back and Coralee poked her head out. Her eyes were red and swollen.

"Can I help you?" she asked weakly.

"No. No, I just... I wanted to see if you were okay." I stumbled over my words.

She sighed and stepped out of the tent.

"Thank you." She dabbed under her eyes with a wad of tissue. "It was just such an awful thing to witness, you know? Seeing my friend like that..." She shook her head.

"I know. I'm so sorry." Dobson put his hand on her shoulder.

"Have you known him long?" I asked.

She nodded. "He's been with this circus longer than I have. He was Elsa's ex-husband, you know." *No, I did not know.* Interesting. She continued, "They didn't get on all that well after the split. Especially once she started seeing Marvin."

"Marvin and Elsa?" I couldn't mask the surprise in my voice. Ferdinand had been quite handsome from what I could tell and Elsa was nothing short of glamorous. Marvin was... well, definitely not a looker.

Coralee nodded and stepped closer like she was about to tell me a secret. "It was after her father died. Some of us suspected she started seeing him because she was worried about pushback from the troupe. She was the new owner, after all. Linking up like that with the ringmaster gave her a little extra bit of control. And everyone loves Marvin. It put her in a very favorable position."

"What happened between her and Ferdinand?" I asked and caught Dobson giving me a look. At first, I thought it read something along the lines of *'Why are you doing my job?'* but he gave me a slight nod and I realized he thought we were making some progress.

"Oh." Coralee rolled her eyes and huffed. "Ferdinand had an eye for every sweet young thing in every town we visited. Elsa just got sick of it, you know? Not that I blame her. Once she finally gave him the boot, he was suddenly a lovesick puppy. She wanted her father to get rid of him but he refused. Ferdinand was too talented, too lucrative." She widened her eyes. "That's another reason I think she started seeing Marvin. Just to piss Ferdinand off. It worked too."

Dobson suddenly looked uncomfortable, staring at the ground and pretending like he was really engrossed in trying to loosen a small rock.

"So why wasn't he fired or whatever once Elsa's dad was gone?"

Coralee shrugged. "I'm not really sure. You'll have to ask Elsa and Marvin."

"Can I ask you one more question?"

She nodded.

"What were you and Marvin arguing about earlier? You seemed really upset."

"Oh." She sighed and waved a dismissive hand in my direction. "I tried to tell him something bad was going to happen. I've been trying to warn him for days. He wouldn't listen. That's all."

"Okay, thanks, Coralee. Are you going to be all right? I think you missed the announcement, but the police asked that everyone stay in their personal trailers for now." I looked at Dobson who had perked up at the word 'police.'

"Yes, that's right, ma'am. I can escort you, if you'd like."

Coralee shook her head. "I can manage. Thanks." She looked back and forth between the two of us like she wanted to say something else, but then she gave a polite smile, "Well, goodnight." She clenched the wad of tissue in her hand and brushed past us toward the row of trailers on the other side of the circus grounds.

Dobson and I started toward the exit again. "You need to tell Harper everything she just told us," I said.

"I know. I'll call him when we get back to your place." He kicked at a rock on the ground. "How come he's mad at you, anyway?"

I felt my stomach lurch and I let out a long breath. "He told me to go home and I didn't."

"He just wants you to be safe."

"Yeah, I know," I said, feeling utterly defeated.

"He cares about you a lot."

"Yeah, he's a good friend."

"I guess. I mean, he *is,* but I don't know if that's it exactly."

"What do you mean?"

"He sure talks about you nonstop. Always seems to have some extra pep in his step when he knows he's going to see you."

"He does?" I tried not to sound too excited at the revelation.

"Yeah. I should probably shut up now though." He giggled. Yes, *giggled*.

I gave Dobson a sidelong glance and saw a knowing smirk pasted on his face. I considered pushing it for a moment but thought better of it. If Harper really did have feelings for me, maybe it was better if I didn't know. I'd been warned by everyone that a relationship with him was off the table. And their logic was solid. Behaving like he was just my friend and telling myself that was all he wanted to be made it easier to ignore my own feelings, which is exactly what I intended to do.

CHAPTER 7

I grabbed the crumpled mess of sheets and blankets from the floor and threw them back onto my bed. "It's gone. It's really gone!" I lay back onto the bed, throwing my arms up over my head in a dramatic fashion.

Maui hopped onto the bed and looked down at me.

"I thought you said you left it on your nightstand?" My mom perched on the head of the antique cherry wood bed frame.

"I did. That's the only place I ever leave it. See that unicorn?" I pointed in the direction of a glittery pink and purple ceramic unicorn without lifting my head from the bed.

"Quite a gaudy thing, isn't it?" Maui mused.

"Hey, my dad bought that for me when I was a kid. It's a ring holder. I always put the ring around the unicorn's horn. I thought maybe I'd set it somewhere else, but there's just no way. I wouldn't do that." I sat up, slumped over in defeat.

"You're sure?" my mom asked.

"I'm sure." I knelt down on the floor again and felt around

under my bed for what the hundredth time. "Why is it called a unicorn anyway? Why not a unihorn?" I wondered aloud.

"A uni…horn?" Maui purred, hopping down onto the floor next to me.

"Yes," I shifted slightly and shoved my hand under the nightstand. "It has one horn, right? So unihorn."

"The prefix *uni* means *unus*, or one, and *cornus* is the Latin word for horn. So unicorn means single horn. So it is a one-horned horse," Maui said.

"Thanks for the linguistics lesson," I mumbled.

"Well, you asked."

My hand brushed against something cold and metallic. "Wait! I found something." I reached farther, my fingers brushing against the object. "It's not a ring though. Too big." I sighed. I finally got a good hold on it and slid it out from under the nightstand.

"What is it?" Mom asked.

"It's a lighter, I think." I held it in my open palm. "One of those fancy ones." It was metal with a flip-top lid and an intricate design on its face.

"Does this belong to Granny?" I asked.

"No, I don't think so. She's always just used matches for lighting candles and such," Mom said.

"Maybe an old suitor's? I mean, it was under the nightstand, after all," Maui teased.

"That's even less likely," my mom said.

"Well, it sure would be nice if she was here so we could ask her about it," I said, not bothering to hide my irritation. I stood, stuffing the lighter in my pocket, and noticed tiny black hairs had fixed themselves to the front of my clothes. I dug around in my nightstand until I found the lint roller. "I really need to sweep in here." I muttered under my breath as I began to methodically remove Maui's hair from my clothes.

"Yes, where was she all night?" Mom asked.

"I don't know. She told me she had plans. Whatever that means. She didn't come home at all last night?"

"Not that I know of," my mom said.

"No. Two nights in a row of peace. It was a dream," Maui said.

"Wait, two nights? She wasn't here the night before? When the clown got killed?" I asked, ripping the top layer of sticky paper from the lint roller and attempting to flick it from my hand.

"No. You didn't know?" He cocked his head to the side.

"No, I didn't. I definitely noticed that we had a quiet night around here. I should've known that was why. And no wonder no one heard anything that night."

"Yes, I got the best sleep of my life that night." Maui stretched, arching his back as he stretched his paws flat in front of him, and lay down on the bed.

"Me too," my mom said, bobbing her head in agreement.

"So did I." I ran the lint roller over my shirt in one final, frenzied attempt. "Which is just way too much of a coincidence."

"What are you thinking?" my mom asked.

"Well," I started to explain but was overcome with irritation and let out a groan instead. "You know I love you, Maui, but what is this?" I held up the lint roller.

He lay on his side in the center of the bed, barely lifting his head before he spoke, "Pardon?"

"What's with all this cat hair? I mean, it's everywhere. All the time." I said in an irritated tone.

He jumped onto his feet and cocked his head. "Since when

do you care about that? I don't know why you've got your knickers in a twist but I've done nothing. Don't start an argy-bargy with me."

"She's just frustrated, Maui." Mom tried to intervene, "But really, sweetheart, you shouldn't take it out on Maui."

"I'm not taking anything out on anyone." I shoved the lint roller back into my nightstand. "Look, I have to go. I'm sorry, Maui. Sometimes I just wish I didn't have black cat hair to contend with all the time." I offered him an apology in the form of a light scratch behind his ear.

He let out a soft purr. "My coat is stunning, thank you very much. And you're quite lucky to get to take a bit of it with you wherever you go."

I laughed, "You're right. You're a beautiful cat. I just meant it would be *easier* if you didn't have it. That's all." I pulled my hand away, satisfied that we'd made up, when the blue smoke began to form around him.

"Dru?" He said in a panicked voice, "Dru, what's happening? What have you done?"

I could hear my mother's voice attempting to calm Maui, but I was too shocked to make out what she was saying. I stood frozen in place and waited for the smoke to dissipate, frightened of what I might've done to my beloved best friend.

It felt like an eternity before the smoke finally began to clear, but what was waiting for me on the other side was far worse than I could've imagined. Maui sat on his backside, his head down as he stared at his hairless body.

"Oh, Maui…" I searched for the right words to say to my fat, wrinkly-skinned, bald cat.

He looked up at me and narrowed his eyes. "Nice one, mate," he hissed. *Yikes.*

"Maui, I am so, so sorry." I took a step toward him but he

lowered his head and glared at me, which was a good sign that it might be best to keep my distance.

"Why do you look so gobsmacked? You did this! Are you having a laugh?" He spat the words.

"Maui, it's my magic. It's... it's not working right." I reminded him. "I didn't mean to. You know that."

"Do I?" He cocked his head to the side.

"Look, I know you're mad. It's completely understandable that you would be." I held my hands up defensively. "But I'm sure there's a lesson to be learned here." I was rambling now, not making any sense.

"A lesson? Did you really just say there's a lesson to be learned here?" His eyes were angry slits now.

"Let's all just take a breath." My mom spoke in her usual soothing tone.

He turned his head to look up at my mom still perched on the bed, "Aurora, look at me. I'm repulsive! I'm... I'm about to throw a wobbly. Oh, bloomin' heck." He gave a quick shake of his head. I wasn't sure what 'throw a wobbly' meant, but I had a feeling it wasn't good.

"No, no. It's not that bad. Really." She tried to sound reassuring.

He jumped from the bed and scampered past me into the living room. In a single bound he was up on the couch and I watched him hesitantly put his two front paws up on the back. He slowly raised his head until he could see himself in the large mirror behind it. He tilted his head to the side and stared at himself for a moment before taking a leap and planting himself on the back of the couch. He stood, examining himself from various angles in the mirror, and I held my breath waiting for him to say something.

71

"See, not that bad." My mom's voice filled the heavy silence of the room.

Maui looked back at us over his shoulder and I felt a pit forming in my stomach. An angry cat was the last thing I needed. Aside from his passive aggressive quips, I'd have to deal with his outright hostility in the form of random attacks on my feet in the middle of the night. He'd wait until I was sound asleep, run at me from across the room, pounce onto the bed, batter my feet in frenzied biting and pawing, and then dash off before I could fully form words in my sleepy state. The next morning he'd pretend as if nothing happened. But I remembered. And it was something I wanted to avoid at all costs. I shuddered at the thought.

"Listen, Maui," I felt a lump in my throat, "it was an accident. You know I'd never do something like this to you on purpose."

"I, for one, think you look handsome." My mom said in such a convincing tone that it made me wonder how often she lied to me too.

Maui turned his head back towards the mirror. "While I *am* proper gutted... I suppose it's not the worst thing you could've done." He arched his back to suck in his round stomach. "It does seem that I've embraced the 'fat and happy' lifestyle quite well though, one might say."

"Is that a good thing?" I asked cautiously.

"Oh, certainly." He jumped from the couch and was back on the bed and staring up at me in a few single leaps. "Now, how are you going to fix this." It was a statement, not a question.

"Well, I'm not sure I can exactly."

He started to protest.

"*But* it should wear off soon. Remember the rats?"

He gasped. "I have to stay like this? You really cocked this up, woman. You really did."

I wasn't going to be able to appease him and I didn't have time to go around in circles anymore. I let out a deep sigh and resolved myself to the reality that I'd have to take my nightly foot attacks as punishment.

"Maui, I'm sorry. I really am. Please forgive me. But I have to go."

His mouth hung open in disbelief.

"I'm sorry." I shrugged and started to turn.

"Wait!" He shouted.

I winced and turned back to face him.

He nudged at the pile of blankets on the bed. "At least cover me up before you go. I am naked, after all. And cold." He said in a miserable voice, no doubt trying to force me to feel guilty. It worked.

I tucked him up in my favorite fleece blanket until only his face peeked out at me. "I really am sorry, Maui. Are you okay?"

"Yes. Just hunky-dory." He said in a sarcastic tone.

"Great." I ignored his sarcasm and hurried to the table next to the front door to grab my cell phone and keys. "Listen, I have to go. If Granny comes back, tell her to come find me."

"Where are you going? Is everything all right?" My mom asked concerned.

"Last night, we discovered that there's a bard with the circus. My ring is missing, we all slept like logs the other night. It's just all too coincidental," I explained.

"Dru, wait." My mom hopped from the bed and flew toward me. She fluttered in the air for a moment before landing on the table.

"There's something you should know." She hesitated.

CHAPTER 8

"I'm listening."

"My father…" her voice trailed off.

"Yes?" I said, growing impatient.

"My father—" she started again.

"Dru!" A frantic voice could be heard over banging against the private door from my apartment into the bookstore.

I hurried to answer and found Tilly standing on the other side. She was wide-eyed, her dyed red hair a ruffled mess. The store had only been open for ten minutes. What could possibly have happened already?

"Tilly, what's wrong?"

"Chickens!" she gasped, out of breath. "Come on! What are you waiting for!?" She grabbed me by the wrist and dragged me down the creaky wooden steps behind her.

Nothing could've prepared me for what I saw when we entered the bookstore. *Chickens.* I know—Tilly had told me. But there were a dozen chickens running amok in the shop. Books were knocked from their shelves, colored crystals were strewn about, statues and a table had been tipped over. And the feathers and chicken poop everywhere…

"What in the…?"

"What do we do?" Tilly asked. I noticed a spot of chicken poop on her pant leg but decided now might not be the best time to tell her.

"How?" It was all I could manage.

"I don't know!" she said in a panic. "We got here this morning and they were just here."

"They're Gloria Powders' chickens, I think." Eve was circling around the store, her arms spread wide, with burning sage in both hands.

"What are you doing?"

"There's obviously evil lurking here," she said in her monotone voice. "I'm cleansing."

"Okay, well, could we maybe deal with the chickens first? I feel like that's the obvious priority." I walked to the center of the store and looked around. There were at least ten that I could count, all talking at once in a mass hysteria.

"Ladies!" I yelled, but it was no use, their frantic cries and confusion drowned out my voice.

We needed to get them out, but I had no idea how.

"Can't one of you just use magic to fix this?" I asked.

"Pete is bringing over Augustus." Eve continued to twirl, her flowy skirt dancing around her. Augustus was their sheepdog.

"So Augustus will what? Chase them out?" I asked.

"Yes," Eve said.

"And then what? Has anyone called Mrs. Powders?" Gloria Powders had just lost her son, one of the only two lawyers in town, and she had taken to collecting even more chickens than she'd started out with.

"I'll ring her." Tilly grabbed the phone from the counter and started flipping through the old fashioned Rolodex we kept.

A chicken squawked and made its way toward her, running straight into her leg. She let out a yelp and shooed it away to the sound of Eve's laughter.

At that moment, the front door swung open. Harper froze mid-way through the doorway and stared wide-eyed. I watched a range of emotions cross over his face but he finally settled on confusion.

"Come on in!" I yelled above the squawking chickens.

He took a few cautious steps toward me, keeping his eyes on the frantic chickens.

"I know you like to host hen parties here, but I think you're taking the gag a little too far." He circled around the front counter and sat down on the stool we kept there.

"Oh, very funny." I gave him a playful shove. "So how did it go last night?"

He opened his mouth but I cut him off.

"Actually, I need to tell you some things first."

"All right. Hit me." He crossed his arms over his chest.

"First, did Dobson tell you about Coralee? Our conversation with her last night?"

He nodded.

"Do Elsa and Marvin have decent alibis?" I asked.

"That's the thing with small, tight-knit groups like these. They all have decent alibis because they all vouch for each other. It's just a matter of discovering who is telling the truth and who is lying. Which can be tougher than you'd think."

I hadn't heard the door open and the sudden burst of even higher-pitched squawking and hysterical cries from the chickens startled me. I looked over and saw Augustus. He was motionless, his head low, but I swore I saw pure joy on his face.

"Hi, Augustus," I called out.

"Hello, Dru," he said in a sly voice before he became nothing more than a blur of white-and-black-spotted gray fur running around the store after the chickens. Their incessant squabbling and confusion were almost deafening and I instinctively put my hands over my ears. That didn't work of course, because you know... we communicate telepathically.

"Are you okay?" Harper stood.

"The chickens." I grimaced.

He gently squeezed my arm and led me through the backdoor into the alleyway behind the store.

"Better?" He asked.

"Much." I pulled the door closed behind me just as I heard *'Faster Franny, he's going to eat us alllll!'*

"That door's been broken into again." Harper examined the doorknob.

"Again!?" I asked in disbelief.

He turned back to me and nodded.

"So, what? The chickens broke in?" I joked.

"You know, if there's one thing I've learned, it's that there's never a dull moment with you." The corner of his mouth turned up in a half smile.

"There used to be. Even when I was a private investigator, my life was pretty boring. I think it's Blackwood Bay that's exciting."

"Oh, I think you're pretty exciting." He winked and I felt my cheeks flush.

"Anyway," I twirled a lock of hair around my finger nervously. "What I was trying to tell you in there was this. You remember the bard from last night, right?"

He nodded.

"And you remember the other night when the clown was

killed, none of us heard anything during the murder *or* when my store was broken into, which is strange because usually at least someone is up no matter what time it is?"

He nodded again.

"Well, I thought I'd misplaced my ring, but now I'm certain he stole it."

"Wait. Back up. Your ring?"

"Yes."

He knit his brow together and scratched at the stubble on his chin. "Why didn't you tell me your ring was missing?"

"I didn't *know* it was missing. I took it off the other night—I do that sometimes—and I thought it was just lost somewhere. But listen, this morning—"

"Dru, you have to tell me when things like this happen." He straightened and rested his hands on his duty belt.

"I have to tell you every time I lose something?"

"You know what I mean. Your ring is a little more important than just *something*."

"Okay, whatever. Listen—"

"Dru, I'm serious. Don't blow me off."

"I'm not blowing you off—" I started, but a crackling from Harper's radio interrupted me.

"Just a minute." He held up a finger and I waited impatiently as Chief Carver's voice came over the radio.

"You might wanna get down here sooner rather than later," Carver was saying. "Seems the ringleader fella was having an affair with one of the other circus performers. Lookin' more like a zoo than a circus here at the moment."

"On my way," Harper said into his radio before looking back at me. "Look, Dru, I have to go. But we'll talk later okay?"

"I think the bard stole my ring," I blurted out.

He looked a little taken aback. "You think he's the one who broke in? To steal it?"

"Yes," I said firmly.

He knit his brow together. "All right. I'll talk to him."

"You'll talk to him?" I asked exasperated.

"Yes. What else would you have me do?" he asked.

"I don't feel like you're taking me seriously."

"I am."

"I'm telling you that I'm pretty sure the bard stole my ring, which might also mean he's the killer, since Chuckles was murdered and my ring was stolen on the same night. You haven't even let me explain yet *why* I think—"

A crackling came over Harper's radio, interrupting me for the second time. "Sergeant?"

"Look, Dru, I'm sorry. I have to go. I'll send someone over so you can report the break in. We'll talk later, okay?" He didn't wait for me to answer before he started talking into his radio and turned and headed down the alleyway toward Main Street.

CHAPTER 9

I felt a lump in my throat and I wasn't sure if I was angry or hurt. *Both*, I decided as I grabbed ahold of the door handle and yanked it open harder than I intended to. I saw Granny standing in the middle of the bookstore, laughing as she watched a single rogue chicken chase Tilly around a row of bookshelves.

"Granny." Augustus gave a brief greeting as he zoomed past her and herded the final chicken out onto the sidewalk in front of the bookstore. I noticed Gloria Powders wasn't there but instead her house sitter had shown up and he was busy collecting chickens and throwing them into the backseat of his car. From what I'd been told, Gloria had always traveled, but she'd spent less than a week in Blackwood Bay after the death of her son, Mitch.

"Are you just getting in now?" I eyed Granny as she entered the bookstore.

"What are you? My mother?"

"Don't deflect," I said.

"Jeez. What's your problem?"

"Guess that answers my question. If you would've arrived anytime between the hours of midnight and 6 a.m., you would've known exactly what my problem is. Dobson stayed over to keep guard last night. He passed out around midnight and let me tell you, you think my dad snores? He's got nothing on Dobson." I noticed Maui had snuck downstairs to watch the show and I pulled him from the counter and into my arms.

"Are you going to tell me where you were?" I asked. "I know you couldn't have gone far. There seems to be some kind of invisible parameter that keeps us within a certain distance of each other. But I've been thinking about what you could've possibly been doing—"

"Then you've already thought way too much about this."

"Well, I was a little bored last night staring at the ceiling and waiting for ghosts to show up. I had time to think. Anyway, what were you doing?"

"Why?"

"What do you mean why?"

"Why are you so worried about it? Keeping tabs on me."

"Fine. Don't tell me," I said, flustered. "Look, I found something this morning while I was looking for my ring."

"Was it your ring?" she deadpanned.

"No." I pulled the lighter from my pocket. "Do you recognize this?" I held it toward her.

Granny leaned forward and studied the lighter for a moment. "No. Do you know what that symbol is though?"

I shook my head, examining it more closely. The symbol was raised but it had been worn down and the previously shiny metal was dull. It looked similar to an ampersand with a row of lines behind it and serpents swirling around on either side. "No, but I have a pretty good idea."

Tilly and Eve both drew closer, leaning in to see what I was holding.

"Is that a musical note?" Tilly asked, tucking a lock of red hair behind her ear.

Eve, who played the harp, plucked the lighter from my hand and held it up to her eye line. "Yes, it's a treble clef."

"The plot thickens," Granny said.

"I didn't get a chance to tell you all this morning because... chickens, but I think the bard is the one who broke in here. And I think it was to steal my ring."

Tilly gasped. "Oh, that's not good." She had such a knack for stating the obvious.

"Yes. I'm still not entirely sure what that means, but I do know that my ring has gone missing and I found this in my apartment."

"Sneaky bard." Eve grinned. "Also, not too bright."

"Right. If he stole my ring, he doesn't know much about how it works—"

"Because it only works for you," Tilly interrupted.

"Right. But it does mean that he knows who I am. Which is concerning."

"Do you think he's the one that killed the clown the other night?"

"It's a good possibility. But I'm not sure what Ferdinand— the acrobat—has to do with any of this. We just don't have all of the pieces to the puzzle yet. I tried to let Harper know, but I didn't get to tell him everything," I said.

"You seem more irritated than necessary by that fact," Eve raised an eyebrow.

"I guess I feel like he's being a little dismissive, you know. Like he's not taking me seriously."

"You're being paranoid," Granny chimed in.

"I'm not being paranoid, Granny," I said.

"I think you need to tell him how you feel." Tilly gave me a sympathetic look.

"I told him. Or at least I started to, but we were interrupted and he had to leave. So I didn't get to tell him everything."

"No, I mean, how you *feel*." She put a compassionate hand on my arm.

"What are you talking about?" A loose section of hair fell in front of my face and I pulled the bobby pin from my hair.

"Oh, please." Eve rolled her eyes. "You get all doe-eyed and jumpy when he's around."

"That's completely irrelevant right now."

"Is it?" Eve arched an eyebrow.

"Yes, of course it is. We have much bigger things to worry about than what I do or do not feel when it comes to Harper."

"But you should, you know. Maybe not today, but soon," Tilly said.

"I've been told that I'm not supposed to though."

"You're not." She said.

"Okay, then. So let's just drop it." I fidgeted with the bobby pin.

The door to the bookstore opened and four teenage boys sauntered in, mischievous smirks on their faces. I instantly recognized them as the ones from the night before, the ones who'd been rude to Dorothy.

"Good afternoon, ladies," the one who had fallen victim to Dorothy's wrath said. An overly confident swagger and the way he positioned himself in front of the other three made it obvious he fancied himself the leader of the group.

"Can I help you?" Eve asked, busying herself with picking up the crystals that had been casualties in the great chicken invasion.

"What happened in here?" one of the boys murmured, and the three lackeys surveyed the destruction.

Mr. Too Cool, however, zeroed in on me instead. "Wow. You have really beautiful eyes, you know that?" He attempted to flatter me as he leaned one elbow against the glass countertop. He was good looking, I'll give him that, but his arrogant demeanor made me think he was using it to cover up some serious insecurities.

"Don't lean on the counter. Not unless you want an arm full of glass shards," I said, ignoring his compliment.

He stepped back and held up his hands defensively, "Sorry. Never met a woman before who didn't like compliments."

I snickered and his friends looked at each other anxiously.

"What can we do for you?" I asked in an intentionally impatient tone.

"Well, I was hoping you might sell spirit boards in here."

"Spirit boards?"

"Yeah, you know. It kind of looks like a board game but it has letters and stuff on it. You can use it to communicate with, like, ghosts and stuff."

"Why do you want to communicate with ghosts?" I crossed my arms.

"Do you question all of your clientele about their purchases? Is this because we're teenagers? That's called ageism, I think, and it's illegal. But I can assure you, *ma'am*, we'll use it very responsibly."

His friends stifled their laughter and he turned and smacked one of them in the stomach.

"Come on." I rolled my eyes, "I don't appreciate hecklers bothering me in my place of business. You need to go." I pointed toward the door.

"Wait. No, I'm serious. We really do want one," he said in a hurried tone, dropping the smooth act.

I placed my hands on my hips and waited for an explanation that would inevitably come if I gave him the silent treatment.

"Look, you heard about those circus guys, right? That clown got killed and then the other guy died last night. We were there. We were just thinking… I don't know. Maybe we could like, communicate with him or something."

"Seriously?" I asked.

He nodded.

"All right, first of all, no, we don't have Spirit Boards. And even if we did, I wouldn't sell you idiots one. You'd probably end up conjuring up the devil or something. And second of all, didn't you all get enough of a show last night watching that poor man fall to his death? You really want to relive it by harassing his ghost?"

"We didn't actually see it though. I mean, we were there, at the circus. But we missed the, you know, death."

"Like you weren't paying attention or something?"

"No. We weren't in the tent when the show started. We got stuck getting a reading or whatever from that weirdo psychic lady. She was a total fake, by the way. We were in there when we heard all the screaming and stuff."

"Wait. You were with the psychic when the acrobat accident happened?"

"Yeah." He sounded disappointed. Interesting. That is *not* what Coralee had told me. I sized all four boys up. Granted, they were dumb and uncouth and had a creepy fascination with Ferdinand's death, but I didn't think they really had a reason to lie to me about being with Coralee. That meant Coralee had lied. But why?

~

*W*e stood in thoughtful silence and I continued to fidget with the bobby pin that I had yet to shove back in my hair.

"I didn't even get to tell Harper about the lighter. That's pretty significant," I said, thinking aloud. "And now with this new information about the psychic. I'm just going to text him and then I'll leave it be. He can figure everything else out on his own." I placed the bobby pin between my lips, slid my cell phone out of my back pocket, and found Harper's number in my contact list. I typed in a short message.

Found a piece of evidence inside my apartment. Also something I need to tell you about the psychic. Thought you'd want to know.

I hit send and heard a ding chime from behind the counter. Tilly braced herself on the glass top and hoisted herself up enough to peer over it. "Uh oh," she said. "Seems he left his phone here."

"It must've fallen out of his pocket." I walked around the side of the counter and picked his phone up from the floor.

"Now what?" Granny was staring at me intently.

"Now what?" I repeated.

Tilly and Eve both stared back at me expectantly.

"He needs to know, I think." I drummed my fingers on the counter. "If the lighter belongs to the bard, then he's the one who was in my apartment and the one who stole my ring."

"On the same night that someone was murdered right outside," Tilly finished.

"Right. And that's information that Harper really needs to have for the investigation." I glanced at the clock on the wall. "And he probably needs his cell phone too, right?"

"I'm sure he'll come back for it as soon as he realizes it's missing." Eve knew what I was thinking and, as usual, slipped right into the role of devil's advocate.

"He's probably crazy busy though. Who knows when he'll realize it's gone? And he might waste time looking for it if he thinks it fell out of his pocket sometime between last night and today," I countered.

"Fine. Go." Eve shook her head but gave me a half smile.

"Thanks. And Eve? Can you have Pete fix the backdoor again? It was broken into again last night."

"The chickens broke in?" Tilly widened her eyes.

"Of course." Eve laughed.

I took a quick scan of the bookstore still in complete disarray. "I'll help you two clean up when I get back. I won't be gone long."

"Oh, don't worry about that." Eve waved her hand, "We'll just call the cleaning fairies."

"Ha!" I let out a short burst of laughter, "If only that were a thing."

Tilly and Eve glanced at each other and then back at me, confusion on both of their faces.

"What?" I looked back and forth between the two of them.

"Are you joshing us?" Tilly crossed her arms over her chest.

"About what?" I asked in confusion.

Eve clasped her hands together under her chin, "Dru, sweetie, do you not know about the cleaning fairies?"

"Very funny." I rolled my eyes and started for the door.

"No, dear. We're being serious." Tilly said.

I whirled around to face them. "About cleaning fairies?"

"Yes, you really don't know about them?" She asked with a worried look on her face.

I most certainly did *not* know about any cleaning fairies. "Are you joking? Because I'm really not in the mood."

Tilly gave a firm nod, "The cleaning fairies are very real. I would never joke about such a thing."

What?! I shook my head, trying to make sense of what they were saying, "Wait. So there's fairies that will come and clean *for* me?"

Eve let out a deep laugh, "Poor thing. Have you really been cleaning everything yourself this whole time?"

"Yes!" I was incredulous. "I wondered how you all were able to get the store closed down and leave it absolutely sparkling clean so quickly. So you're telling me what? That little fairies just come every time and do it for you?"

"I think we just blew her mind." Eve grinned and nudged Tilly with her elbow.

"I'm sorry." Tilly glanced at Eve. "We just assumed someone had told you about them."

"No." I shot daggers in Granny's direction.

"Oops." She said with a quick shrug of her shoulders.

"They aren't fairies exactly. That's just what we call them." Eve was saying, "They're actually a coven of tiny, little witches that live in the woods. But yes, they love to clean. I mean, *love* it. They're inexplicably strong too. And sure, you can use your magic, but it's still so time consuming, you know?"

In the month since I'd found out I was a witch, I had yet to come to the obvious conclusion that I could use my magic to clean and I grimaced at my own stupidity.

Eve prattled on, "If you want a thorough job though, you call the cleaning fairies. They do laundry, toilets, everything."

"Oh, my god!" I groaned. "How did I not know about this?"

"Sorry." Tilly offered.

I considered the idea of having adorable little witches come and clean while I lay as a lazy lump on the couch and watched them, and I was suddenly overcome with excitement.

"Don't be sorry. This is fantastic news!" I grabbed Tilly up in an enthusiastic embrace and planted a firm kiss on her cheek.

Eve laughed, "See, I told you we blew her mind."

"Listen, I have to go." I said pulling back, "But we are definitely going to talk more about this later." I started for the door.

"*W*ell, I'm not letting you go alone. Especially since you aren't armed with your magic," Granny said resolutely.

"Be careful!" Tilly called out.

"I will. I'll be right back. I'm just going to drop this off and I'll be back in no time."

That would prove to be a lie, but I meant it when I said it.

CHAPTER 10

*G*ranny and I neared the entrance of the circus, walking in silence. Empty paper cups and circus flyers littered the ground and a slight breeze from the bay kicked up dust as it passed. Last night, it had been filled with music and lights and laughter and, in my personal opinion, a slight horror movie vibe, but today it was akin to a ghost town from an old western movie. I half expected two gunslingers to swagger out from opposite sides and challenge each other to a quick draw duel. But there was another feeling that suddenly took over. An eerie feeling that, in spite of not seeing a soul in site, someone was watching me. It sent a shiver down my spine.

"Are you all right?" Granny asked.

"Yeah, fine," I said curtly.

"No, you're not."

I sighed. "I'm just…"

"I'm worried about you.," she said.

"You are?"

"Of course I am." She seemed genuinely surprised by my doubt.

"I'm fine, Granny," I said in a quiet voice.

"You don't have to talk to me about it. But you should talk to him."

I knew exactly what she meant. "I will."

"While we're here, I'm going to go snoop around. If you see the bard and you're alone, go the other way," she said.

"Okay, but I'm *just* giving Harper his phone and then I'm out of here."

She smirked. "Okay. We'll see." And she was gone.

The unsettling feeling of being watched returned and I quickened my pace, looking for a sign of life, but not finding any. The performers kept their trailers separate from the main circus grounds, behind thick layers of rope and chain to ward off guests who might try and wander away from the designated entertainment area. I guessed that Harper was amidst the trailers somewhere, probably questioning suspects and witnesses, so I made my way back. Feeling increasingly uncomfortable as I went, I decided to sneak around to the opposite side of the trailers, out of the direct view of anyone. I heard distant voices and figured I was headed in the right direction.

The first trailer I passed had its curtains drawn, but the second had its wide open. I slowed as I passed, peeking inside. It was decorated in bright, sunny colors, yellows and reds, and the walls were lined with vintage movie posters. Continuing on, I saw a weathered wooden sign adhered to the door. *Curly* was etched deep into the wood and a dark varnish settled into the letters. I took a few steps to my right and looked down at the rows of trailers. Each had a name on its door.

I glanced around, but I seemed to be alone. There were two clear options here: continue on, find Harper, give him his phone, and leave. Or snoop around.

The second option had far more potential to be dangerous—and possibly illegal.

But I desperately wanted to find my ring and unmask a killer in the process. Also, as previously mentioned, I'm nosy.

I crouched down and made my way forward, looking underneath the trailers to check for any feet on the other side, until I reached the one I was looking for.

Ridley, it read in the same childlike font as the others.

I stopped and looked around and listened for a moment for footsteps or voices. Satisfied that I was alone, I stood on my tiptoes and peeked inside the window. He had dark curtains drawn, black, which was no surprise, but they were slightly off as if he'd thrown them shut haphazardly in a hurry. I squinted through the window's glare. It looked pretty bare. A pullout couch in a '70s orange floral pattern, a small kitchen with an old mini-fridge. Nothing hung on the walls, and the counter and table were clear except for a single coffee mug.

I sighed, disappointed, not sure what I thought I'd find. While I wasn't expecting a sign on the wall itemizing all of his crimes, I'd still hoped for something interesting. If he did have my ring, he would've hidden it though.

That meant I needed to do some digging.

I sank back down on my heels and took a quick look around. Still alone. I grasped the handle and yanked, and it popped right open. *Guess I'm really doing this now.* I took one hesitant step up, aging metal creaking under the weight of my foot. I winced at the noise and scanned the area. Nothing. I leaned my head inside, keeping both of my feet firmly planted on the step. I looked to the left and saw that everything I had been able to see through the window was all there was. Couch, kitchen, coffee mug. It was almost as if no one really lived there. I looked to the right and saw a closed door.

His bedroom? Now that was guaranteed to have something in it.

I hesitated. This was a bad idea. I knew it. It was dangerous and stupid and Granny and Harper would both kill me.

But something drew me to it. My ring? Could it be that my ring was drawing me to it? And if so, that was as good of an excuse as any, right? I reasoned with myself that I would just peak in. Just open the door. If I didn't feel the pull of my ring, then I was out of there.

I stepped inside the tiny trailer that smelled oddly of peppermint. The carpet was low pile, the kind you'd see in school classroom, and a hideous green that clashed with the orange colored couch. The floor creaked under my footsteps and a thought occurred to me. *What if he was here and he hasn't come to the door because he's sleeping?* I paused.

He was a bard, which meant he could perform magic. But he had to use music to do it. I was a witch. Granted, my magic was out of control at the moment. But surely some magic that I could use at will had to be able to overpower a guy that needed a harmonica to perform his.

Feeling a sudden swell of courage, most likely misplaced, I continued toward the door. I turned the knob slowly, holding my breath as I eked it open. When it was far enough to stick my head in, I did just that.

The bed was empty. Perfectly made up like the bard had spent years working as a hotel maid, the blue blanket perfectly was tucked under the mattress and pillows. I wedged the door open a tiny bit further to peer in past it. A small nightstand. Empty. A metal cage. A row of black suits.

Wait… my eyes darted back. *A metal cage?*

I squinted my eyes like that would help me understand what

I was looking at. A large cage with thick metal bars sat in the corner of the room, taking up half of the space.

I had a wire travel carrier for Maui and I'd seen plenty of cages and carriers for animals, but this was something else. It stood at least five feet tall, the bars were a thick steel, at least three inches in diameter with less than a few inches between them. There was a small door with three separate padlocks on it like the ones I'd had for my gym lockers in school. I grimaced at the sudden flashback. There was no mat or blankets on the floor of the thing either.

I was perplexed. This circus had no animals. And a pet the size that would fit into this thing would be hard to miss. What was this for? A sudden pit formed in my stomach and the urge to run overwhelmed me.

Turning and bolting from the trailer, I slammed the door behind me without even considering that someone might've seen me. I did a great job sneaking in and a completely amateur job sneaking out. I hurried around the back side of Ridley's trailer and out into the main communal area and spotted Harper and Dobson stepping out from behind a trailer.

A sense of relief instantly washed over me.

We made eye contact and he paused for a moment, no doubt surprised to see me. I watched him turn and say something to Dobson before he strode over to me. Unable to read the look on his face, I resolved myself to keep the interaction short and sweet.

I pulled his phone from my pocket, blurting out the words before he'd actually reached me. "You dropped this at the bookstore." I held out his phone like a sacrificial offering and stared at it in my hand.

"Oh, thanks. I didn't even realize it was missing. Been more than a little crazy around here today." He reached out for the phone, brushing my fingertips as he did, and I let go a second too soon. *Smooth, Dru.* His phone bounced to the ground, throwing up dust.

"I'm sorry." I bent down to pick it up and smacked my head into his.

I yelped—also not attractive—and grabbed my head as I stood back up. Harper had secured his phone, but he held a hand over one eye.

"That's definitely going to leave a mark." He grinned, showing off his dimples. "Thanks for bringing it by. You didn't have to do that."

"It's no problem." I hesitated.

"All right, well, I should get back." He motioned over his shoulder.

"Sure." I gave a slight wave and folded my arms over my chest.

He studied me for a moment like he was waiting for something, but after a few seconds he turned to walk away.

"Wait!" I blurted out.

He spun around, a smile tugging at the edges of his lips. "I knew it."

A short burst of nervous laughter escaped my lips. "This morning, some teenagers came in, right after you left, and long story short, Coralee did *not* see Ferdinand fall last night." I paused for effect.

He knit his brow together and I saw his eye was already beginning to swell.

"Harper! That means she lied. She told Dobson and I she did, but she didn't."

"According to some teenagers?" he asked.

"Yes," I said in an irritated tone, "but why would they lie?"

"I'm not saying they did. But they may have gotten some of

the details mixed up. And we also have to assume everyone is lying for now."

I sighed. "Fine. Okay, second thing." I looked around and lowered my voice to barely above a whisper. "I already told you about the bard and how I think he stole my ring for some reason. But I didn't tell you *why* I thought that."

"It doesn't really matter." He said, squinting through his bad eye.

"What do you mean it doesn't matter?"

"I mean we're working on a double homicide. He was most likely at the scene of the crime for the first murder, if he was the one who broke in, and he had opportunity for the second. We haven't worked out a motive yet, but that doesn't really matter either. Right now, we're talking to everyone and trying to gather evidence."

"That's what I'm trying to give you!" I was exasperated at that point.

"Whoa, Dru. Calm down. Why are you mad?" He held up his hands defensively.

"Why am I mad?" I huffed. "Because I've been trying to share information with you, *trying* to give you possible evidence, *trying* to help you, and you keep blowing me off. *And* you told me you needed my help today but you blew that off too." I felt my voice crack on that last word.

Oh no, no. I was *not* going to cry.

After I caught my ex-fiancé Jason cheating on me with my best friend, I vowed that I would never let another man see me cry again. I couldn't break that vow today. Not here. Not in this dusty, trash-covered field. And not in front of this man who I was most certainly falling for but who had no idea.

"Dru, I'm sorry." He took a step toward me. "I'm so sorry if you felt I was blowing you off. I would never, ever. I'm doing the best I can. Trying to keep you safe, doing my job, and trying to navigate this—" he motioned to me and then to himself.

"Sergeant!"

Harper whirled around and I saw Chief Carver urgently waving his arms in the air. Once he determined Harper had seen him, he spun around and took off toward the rows of trailers, other police officers coming out from random hiding spots and running behind him.

Harper turned back to me. "Get home, Dru. Go. Hurry. I'll call you as soon as I can." He took off after Chief Carver and left me standing there in his literal dust.

I sighed, still frustrated with the fact that I was still carrying the lighter around in my pocket despite trying to give it to Harper twice now. I turned back the way I'd came, walking at a slow pace so I could look for Granny without being too obvious. I started to consider what Chief Carver might've found that caused such a reaction out of him. I hadn't known him long, but he was basically every small town sheriff you've ever seen on TV. One of those strong, silent types, he was never in much of a hurry. Whatever it was, it must've been pretty serious, and I hoped it would lead to catching the killer.

I rounded the corner past the entrance and a smaller tent that had housed the concession stand the night before, when I almost ran smack into someone.

CHAPTER 11

I shrieked. He whirled around and I recognized him as Jimmy, the tall clown from the night before.

"Sorry," I said, my heart still pounding.

"No worries. Circus is closed today though, ma'am."

I had two options: tell him what I was really doing there, or play dumb to fish for some new information. Of course I went with option two.

"Oh, it is? Gosh, I wondered why I didn't see anyone else. Why are you closed?"

"Had an accident here last night. You didn't hear?" Lucky, the little person, spoke up.

"No." I shook my head. "What happened? Is everyone all right?"

"'Fraid not. One of our acrobats died," Jimmy said.

"Oh, gosh! That's just terrible. You said an accident. Did that person die during the performance?"

They both nodded and I caught the fire-eating woman wiping at her eyes.

"Trapeze broke," Lucky said, stuffing his hands further down in his pockets.

"Oh, no. I'm so sorry."

"Yup. A real loss." Jimmy hung his head.

"What a terrible accident," I said.

"Well, not exactly an accident." Lucky scrunched his face up. "Somebody messed with it."

I gasped, pressing my hand to my chest for the full dramatic effect. Wow, was I good or what?

"We all know who it was too." The fire-eating woman stood, her voice trembling with emotion.

Here we go.

Jimmy nodded. "You're right there, Grace. Not sure how we'll prove it though."

"We don't need to prove it! That's the cops' job." Lucky spat. "She's the only one with a reason to want him dead though. We all know that."

"Yeah, but what if the police don't believe us? We told them everything, but she hasn't been arrested. She's still wandering around here with her nose in the air," the fire-eating woman, apparently named Grace, said.

"Who?" I asked.

Lucky scrunched up his face again and in a mocking tone said, "The beautiful Elsa Braun."

CHAPTER 12

"*E*lsa Braun?" Keeping the act going, I pretended like I didn't know who she was.

"She owns this circus. Well, she thinks she does. What she actually owns is all the equipment and the name. She inherited both of 'em when her father died." Lucky smirked.

"Why do you think she killed Ferdinand?"

"He was her ex. She hated him but he wouldn't leave, and Marvin was too much of a chicken to get rid of him. Probably 'cause he knew we'd all boycott if he did."

"He tried real hard to push her out too," Jimmy chimed in, pulling a cigarette from a pack in his shirt pocket.

"What do you mean, tried to push her out?"

Grace spoke up. "Oh, you know, tried to make her life a living hell. I mean, she's the owner in name, but he wanted her to sell to him. He helped her father build this circus from the ground up too. She refused, and that's when he started the psychological warfare."

"Finally pushed her to the edge, I think. Marvin too," Jimmy said quietly.

"Wouldn't surprise me," Lucky agreed.

Grace let out a strangled laugh. "That was before she found out Marvin is just as big of a sleazeball as Ferdinand was. Bet she's starting to regret it now."

Jimmy and Lucky both shook their heads.

"I still can't believe Coralee was dumb enough to fall for Marvin. What could she possibly see in him?" Grace smirked.

"Wait. Coralee and Marvin?" I blurted out.

All three of them narrowed their eyes at me.

"I mean—I know Marvin is the ringleader. Who's Coralee?" I finished up quickly.

"She's the psychic around here." Jimmy softened his gaze. "Well, she says she is."

"You really think they did it?" I hadn't really noticed him before, but there was another little person sitting by himself on an overturned bucket.

"Oh, didn't see ya there, Curly." Lucky's cheeks grew an obvious shade of pink.

"That's Curly. Elsa is his mom," Jimmy said gently.

"Ah, you know, don't know who else it could've been, really," Lucky said, awkwardly shuffling his feet.

"Ridley," Jimmy said under his breath. Ridley, the magician, the bard.

"Who's Ridley?" I asked.

"No one knows," Lucky joked.

"He's been with us a long time. Keeps to himself though. Kind of a jerk, if you wanna know the truth," Jimmy said. Yeah, definitely got that vibe from him myself. "One of those real, uh, psychopathic types."

"Pretentious," Grace corrected, taking a long drag from a cigarette. Eh, either one could probably fit.

"Ridley's not a jerk." Curly stood up, the sunlight bouncing off of his mop of orange hair. I took a sidelong glance at Grace, trying to determine if she was smoking a Tennessee King, but she caught me and I turned my attention back to Curly.

"I know you like him, pal," Jimmy said in a kind tone before turning to me. "Ridley, he's just kind of an odd guy, you know. Hard to befriend, kind of a loner. His only real friends here are Curly and Chuckles."

"Chuckles?" I feigned ignorance.

"Yeah, you might've heard about it. Someone killed him two nights ago in town. He and Ridley were good friends."

That complicated things slightly. If Chuckles was Ridley's friend, then there was a possibility that Ridley, though a thief, was not a murderer.

"Wow. And none of you saw anything suspicious that night?"

"No. We were all together." Lucky motioned to Jimmy and Grace. "Curly had food poisoning so he spent all night in his trailer."

"Why would anyone want to kill Chuckles though?" I asked.

They all looked around at each other, but no one spoke.

"Did he have issues with Elsa too?" I prodded.

"She didn't like him much," Lucky finally said.

"Chuckles drank. A lot," Grace offered. That didn't really seem like a decent motive for murder, but no one supplied any further explanation.

I was contemplating my next question when I saw movement a few yards past Jimmy and realized it was Granny trying to flag me down.

"Well, thanks. And uh, I'm sorry about what's happened," I said and started past them toward Granny.

"Where you going?" Lucky took a step in front of me.

"Oh, just need to use the bathroom real quick. I walked all the way here and there's no way I'll make it home." I feigned a shy smile.

"Oh, all right then." He nodded and stepped out of my way.

I hurried in Granny's direction, looking around for Harper or the bard.

"Found him!" She beamed.

"Who?" I whispered.

"The acrobat." She started walking before I'd even caught up to her.

"No Chuckles?" I whispered.

"Nah. Don't know where that clown is hiding. But maybe Ferdinand can give us something."

"I hope so." I let out a deep exhale and followed Granny, glancing back over my shoulder to make sure no one was following us. We slipped back behind a small red tent and saw Ferdinand standing with his back to us. He turned when he saw us approaching and I noted that Granny hadn't been kidding about the ghost uniform bit. He still wore the bizarre pastel blue costume that showed off his muscular physique, amongst other things.

He was handsome in the way that men with boyish features are, but as I got closer, I noticed that his dark hair was accented with wisps of gray and he had lines that crinkled at the corners of his eyes when he smiled.

"Ah, this must be her. You didn't tell me your granddaughter was such a beauty." He arched an eyebrow. With a name like Ferdinand, I expected an interesting accent. Maybe French or Spanish. Instead, he spoke with a thick New York accent and it caught me slightly by surprise. "What a gorgeous woman you are. Your eyes, like two pools of honey. Your hair, like the first snow of winter—"

"Can it, Ferdi. We don't have time for you to be hitting on my granddaughter. Besides, you're dead." With that harsh reminder, Granny shut him down.

"What can you tell us about what happened the other night? Do you remember anything that could help?" I asked.

He looked thoughtful for a moment. "Well, I do remember the accident, if that's what you're asking."

"It wasn't an accident though," I said.

The surprise on his features was genuine—or an act so convincing he'd missed his true calling in front of a TV camera. "What are you saying?"

"Someone set you up to die," Granny said matter-of-factly. "You were murdered."

He gasped. "That can't be right!"

"It most certainly is," she replied.

Ferdinand hung his head and placed his hands on his ghostly hips and I couldn't help but feel bad for him. It was probably tough to find out that you'd been murdered.

"Do you have any ideas about who might've wanted to get rid of you?" I asked gently.

He stared at the ground and shook his head. "There's really only one person I can think of."

"Well, who is it?" Granny said impatiently.

"Marvin, of course." He looked up at us. "Elsa is my ex-wife."

"Yes, I heard that," I said.

"And you also heard that Marvin is her new..." He paused and got a look on his face like he'd just tasted something bitter.

"Yes, we knew that too."

"Did you also know that that two-timing, no good slime was cheating on her?" His eyes were wide.

"No offense, but didn't you cheat on her too?" I asked.

He narrowed his eyes at me. "I made mistakes. Mistakes I wish I could take back. After she left me, I nearly killed myself fighting to get her back." He softened his facial expression. "I love her. I really do."

"Okay, you're sorry you cheated, you love her, blah blah. Why would Marvin want you dead?" Ah, Granny, always one to get to the point.

"Because I had an absolute ace up my sleeve and he knew it. I caught the man red-handed. With Coralee. And I was prepared to tell Elsa everything. I was going to wait until after opening night because I didn't want to ruin her performance. I knew she would be upset. And I would be there to comfort her and show her I was a changed man. It would've been perfect." He shook his head. "And now... what do I do now?" His eyes pleaded.

"Let me get back to you when I think of something witty to say," Granny said.

"Some of the other performers told me that you were making things hard on Elsa. Trying to get her to sell to you and just being an all-around jerk."

He took a step back and furrowed his brow. "No. No, that's not... that's not what I was trying to do. I wanted to own this circus *with* her, not take it from her. We built it together, her father and I. I thought if I could continue his legacy and make it as great as it once was, it would prove to her how much I loved her."

"I think less bed-hopping might've been an easier feat," Granny quipped.

"Does *she* think I was trying to get rid of her? Does she think I hated her too?" He looked distressed at the possibility.

"I'm not sure. I haven't spoken with her yet," I answered truthfully.

"I am—was—a stubborn man sometimes. I get an idea in

my head and I run with it, and I don't always think it through first. Maybe I did give everyone the wrong impression. But I thought Elsa would've understood what I was trying to do. She knew me better than anyone."

"Thanks, Ferdinand," I said.

"What about Chuckles though? What would he have to do with any of this that would've gotten him killed?" Granny asked.

"My guess is that he saw something that night that he wasn't supposed to. And that's what got him killed. Wrong place, wrong time," I answered.

Ferdinand opened his mouth to speak, when a blood-curdling scream erupted through the air—a scream so pained that it sent a chill up my spine.

CHAPTER 13

*A*ll three of us raced toward the sound of the screaming that continued to rip through the circus grounds. Crew members and performers had the same idea and we all converged in the center of the manmade pathway. I spotted the performers I had spoken to earlier and received a few suspicious looks.

Just as we approached the row of trailers, the screaming stopped and in its place came pained sobs. I saw Harper and Chief Carver directing officers and Dobson was on the ground, holding a crumpled Elsa in his arms. All of us stopped dead in our tracks, watching the scene in front of us and trying to determine what had happened. Ferdinand was the only one to continue on, kneeling down in front of Elsa. He watched her intently and tried to smooth her hair with his hand.

I realized how quiet it was, nothing but the sounds of sobs and hushed speaking between police officers, when suddenly curses where being hurled through the air.

Coralee was trying to push past a police officer who'd cornered her just a few yards away.

"She killed him!" She was screaming. Her eyes were wild and she threw her arms about, directing her words at those of us standing on the opposite side. "I caught her! Standing over him with a knife in his back!" she yelled. Elsa continued to rock rhythmically with Dobson, as if she hadn't heard Coralee's accusations.

The officer tasked with controlling Coralee was attempting to hang onto her around the waist as she wriggled against his embrace.

"Didn't you all hear me? Do something! She killed him!" she screamed, her voice taking on a guttural sound.

"Who?" someone shouted from behind me.

"Marvin! She killed Marvin!"

I heard audible gasps all around me and looked to Elsa for her reaction. It took her a few seconds, as if there was a delay and things were only just beginning to register. But she stopped rocking and pulled away from Dobson, who widened his eyes in anticipation. She wiped under her eyes, though it only smeared the black mascara even more, giving her a terrifying look. She stood, leaning on Dobson for support, and smoothed down the front of her dress as if she was attempting to put herself back together. Dobson stood next to her and cautiously looked back and forth between her and Coralee.

"Uh-oh." Ferdinand looked at Granny and me.

"I beg your pardon?" she finally spoke, her voice shaky.

"You killed him! I saw you!" Coralee shouted, straining against the police officer's grip.

"I most certainly did not," she said calmly. "I found him, yes. But I did not kill him."

"Liar!" Coralee screamed. "I saw you standing over him with a knife in his back!" She started to cry.

"I'm a liar?" Elsa narrowed her eyes. "I'm a liar?" She took a step forward and Dobson did the same. "You are the one who was sleeping with him behind my back! You are the liar! Both of you!" She was yelling now, her usual stoic demeanor completely absent in the heat of the moment.

"Don't turn this around on me, you murderer!"

"Hey, leave her alone!" Ferdinand yelled.

"I didn't kill him!" Elsa lunged forward, Dobson grabbing her around the waist.

"I saw the knife sticking out of his back. I saw you standing over him."

"I found him that way."

"How convenient." She snarled and directed her gaze at Carver and Harper. "I'm sure you'd be happy to know that the knife belongs to her too."

Carver and Harper exchanged glances.

"Some stupid family heirloom or something," she announced with a smirk.

I heard a low whistle and turned to see none other than the bard standing directly next to me. He gave a quick raise of his eyebrows and leaned over. "Elsa's father was a knife thrower before he became a ringmaster. She's kept his knife collection on display in her trailer ever since he passed," he whispered. The hair stood up on the back of my neck. I knew there was no way my ring would fit on his finger, but I caught myself glancing down at his hands anyway. He had them stuffed in his pockets.

"Someone obviously stole it and is framing me, you insolent hussy!" Elsa shouted.

"At least I wasn't using Marvin to try to hang on to a dying circus where everyone hates me!"

Elsa looked taken aback and I saw hurt clouding her face.

"What are you doing here anyway?" he asked.

I could feel Granny watching us closely and I was thankful she was there with me.

"Actually, don't answer that question. You'll just lie. And I hate when people lie to me." He straightened back up and turned his attention back to the scene in front of us. I snuck a glance at Granny and she had her brow scrunched up.

Harper and Dobson had begun to break up the fight, two officers pulling Coralee away and telling her if she didn't stop, they'd take her in and let her sit in a cell to cool down. Carver was speaking with Elsa in a hushed tone and suddenly he was leading her away toward the exit. Ferdinand was following close behind.

Harper caught my eye and motioned for me to wait.

"You're probably in trouble," Granny said.

"Probably." I grimaced.

"Sorry?" the bard said and I realized he thought I was talking to him.

"Oh, uh, just talking to myself."

He studied me, the crowd dispersing behind us. I waited for him to say something but instead he turned abruptly and walked away.

I waited until everyone was out of earshot before turning to Granny. "He's creepy," I said under my breath.

"Surprised to still see you here," Harper said as he approached.

"Yeah, sorry. I was actually leaving but then I found Ferdinand. Well, Granny did. And then we heard screaming and well..." I explained.

He narrowed his eyes like he was trying to decide whether he believed me or not.

"Don't you want to know what he told me?" I asked.

"Sure." Harper placed his hands on his hips.

"He said he loved Elsa and that he caught Marvin cheating on her with Coralee. He was going to tell her too. But right before that, I ran into some other performers and they said that Elsa hated him and he'd been making her life a living hell."

Harper nodded.

"So? Did they both have alibis for the night Chuckles died? I mean, I know we don't know exactly when the trapeze was tampered with. But we do know when Chuckles was murdered."

"Well," Harper sighed, "Marvin's alibi was that he was with Coralee. And she corroborated. That's how this all came to a head. They had to cop to the affair. And Elsa found out. And then, as you know, she found him dead in his trailer with a knife in his back."

"So maybe Marvin did kill Chuckles and Ferdinand. And then Elsa found out about the affair and killed Marvin in a rage?" I said in a low voice.

"Or maybe she killed all three of them. Marvin because he broke her heart, Ferdinand because he broke her heart and he wouldn't leave her in peace, and Chuckles because he saw her tampering with the trapeze."

"So she's under arrest?" I asked.

"Carver took her in for questioning. But there's a good chance that it'll end in an arrest." He nodded.

"I don't know," I said.

"Don't know what?"

"Something doesn't feel right about this." The wheels started turning in my head.

Harper massaged his forehead with one hand and rested the other on his hip.

"I mean, think about it." When he didn't speak up, I decided to continue. "Yes, she had motive to kill Marvin. But Ferdinand —I don't know if I buy it, not with the guy still professing his love for her even now. And what about the fight we saw between Coralee and Marvin last night? Did you ask either of them about it? And I still think she lied about seeing Ferdinand fall. We also have someone that broke into my building. Most likely you know who—"

"Dru." Harper held up his hand to stop me.

"What?"

"Stop." He had his eyes closed.

"What do you mean? I'm trying to help you." I folded my arms over my chest defensively.

He let out a deep breath and let his eyes meet mine.

"You told me I could help you. You told me you wanted my help." I kept an even tone.

"You're right. I did. And to be perfectly honest, I shouldn't have. That was stupid. I'm supposed to be doing what's in your best interest, not mine. Asking you to help out with dangerous investigations is selfish."

"Why?"

"Because I'm your guardian—" he started.

"You know, if I have to hear you say that one more time, I'm going to explode." I took a deep breath and a step toward him, ignoring the confused look on his face. "What if I don't want you to be my Guardian? Then what?"

"That's not an option," he said flatly.

"Why not? What's going to happen? Is there some special forces unit made up of fairies and ogres that comes and whisks away magical people and puts them in a secret magical jail?" I said with more anger than I realized had built up inside of me. "And who even decides this stuff anyway? Who picked you?"

"Dru!" Granny scolded and I realized I'd completely forgotten she'd been standing there the whole time. "Enough. He didn't choose you himself."

"Who decided then, huh?" As far as any onlookers were concerned, I was yelling at thin air. Fortunately, there weren't any.

"It's better if I don't tell you. You'll find out when the time is right."

I groaned. "Just like everything else, huh? The information just leaks in a little at a time. Everyone has me on a need-to-know basis." I turned back to Harper, ignoring the hurt in his eyes. "And let me tell you one more thing." I was really on a roll now. "I am *not* that girl, okay? I try to figure things out on my own. I take care of myself. I'm not that girl who goes running into the arms of the first big strong man she sees and asks him to save her."

"Are you done?" he asked, sticking his tongue in his cheek.

Taken aback by his response, I stuttered, "Yes, I think so."

"Good. Go home then." He turned and I watched his broad back move further and further away from me until the tears stung my eyes so much that I had to blink. I turned and started walking, not knowing if Granny was with me and not caring.

CHAPTER 14

"*Y*ou need to go after him and apologize," Granny said sternly.

"Why?" I managed through my tears.

"Because you acted like an ass, that's why," she said.

"I don't need this from you right now," I said, ignoring the confused faces of the people I passed seeing a woman crying and talking to herself.

"Oh, yes, you do. It's exactly what you need right now."

I took a hard right and walked back behind the abandoned concession stand. I turned to face Granny, hardening my resolve. "I meant what I said back there."

"I know you did," she said calmly.

"Then what's there left to discuss?" I raised my chin defiantly.

"Look, you can save the whole strong woman routine for someone else, okay? I get it. But you don't need to treat him poorly because of it. It's not his fault. He's doing what he's supposed to. If you don't like it, keep your distance. You don't need to be friends. Have a normal Guardian-Witch relationship. Except you won't. Because that's not really what you want." She adjusted her glasses.

"How could you possibly know what I want?" I sighed in defeat. "I don't even know what I want."

"Knowing what you want and having what you want are two very different things."

"Fine." I sighed. "You're right."

"If you could just get it through your head that that is a *given* we could save so much time."

"I'm going to apologize." I brushed past Granny and made my way out from behind the concession stand and it appeared that I wouldn't have to go far to find him.

Harper was standing with Dobson and a few of the circus performers who I'd spoken to earlier, his back to me. I started toward him, frantically searching my mind for the right words to say.

"Were you in my trailer?" The velvety voice was so close to my ear that I jumped and let out a shriek.

Granny cursed and I took a few steps back to look at Ridley's smirking face.

"What? Uh... no." I turned to walk away, ready to yell Harper's name.

"You lie a lot. Why do you like lying so much?" He kept pace with me.

"What are you talking about?"

"First you lied about your name. Then you lied about being in my trailer," he said in a cheery voice.

I came to a halt. "What do you mean I lied about my name?"

"Well, I know you're not Tiffany Gold-whatever." He placed his hands in his pockets and leaned back on his heels.

I stared at him blankly, searching my mind for something to say.

"First, the hair is a dead giveaway for anyone that knows who they're supposed to be looking for." He cocked his head to the side.

"Dru, if you need to use your magic, just do it. It'll probably end badly, but we'll clean up that mess later," Granny said.

I nodded. "Why are you looking for me then?" I asked. I heard footsteps to my right and saw Harper approaching out of the corner of my eye. Maybe the whole Guardian thing wasn't such a bad idea after all.

"Everything all right over here?" he asked. The area around his eye was already turning a shade of purple and I felt a pang of guilt tug at my heartstrings.

"Oh, fine, Officer. Just chatting, weren't we?" he said, never taking his eyes off of me.

"Good to hear." Harper grinned and wagged his finger at Ridley. "You know, it's actually really convenient that you're here because I've been looking for you. I just had a few questions." He gave me a quick look before turning his attention back to Ridley.

"You see, my friend here, she owns the building that was broken into the other night. I'm sure you heard. The night that Chuckles was killed, someone broke into the building where he was murdered."

Ridley nodded, but seemed unaffected. "Yes, I did hear something about that."

"I don't recall who questioned you about your alibi for that night."

I moved my hands to bring them up and cross my arms over my chest when I brushed something hard and rectangular in my pocket. *Of course!* The lighter.

"Oh, I assure you, I was questioned thoroughly," Ridley said.

I bent down like I had to tie my shoe, almost making myself look like a complete idiot because I was wearing sandals. Instead, I recovered by adjusting one of my straps and glanced up to make sure neither man was watching me.

"Hmm... humor me." Harper scratched at his five-o-clock shadow.

Ridley smirked. "Your people just hauled Elsa away. Not confident you've caught your man—or woman, in this instance?"

"Ugh. He's so smug," Granny was saying as she watched the scene unfold.

Fishing the lighter from my pocket, I stood up again. "Huh. Is this yours?" I turned to Harper first. He shot me a confused look. I turned to Ridley and held it out.

He leaned forward slightly. "Yes. I lost this days ago. It was just there, lying on the ground?" He furrowed his brow.

"Actually, no. You lost it in my apartment when you broke in."

"Aha!" Granny shouted victoriously.

Ridley looked up at me, his eyes narrowing to angry slits.

"What's going on, sir?" I heard a voice coming up behind Harper. It was Curly and the rest of the performers who'd been so helpful earlier.

"I don't think they're so certain about your mother's involvement anymore." Ridley's eyes bore into me.

"My mom didn't kill anybody. But Ridley didn't either. He was with me all night when Chuckles was killed. And there's no way he could've tampered with the trapeze. I kept watch on it all that day that Ferdinand died," Curly said.

"But earlier, Jimmy said you had food poisoning that night," I spoke up.

Curly shot me a glare.

"Do you have an alibi then?" Harper asked Ridley.

He pulled a cigarette from the pack in his pocket and took his time bringing it to his mouth and lighting it with his newly reacquired lighter. Last night had been too dark to see, but in the daylight, it was glaringly obvious and I felt a sinking sensation in the pit of my stomach. He took a long drag from some generic cigarette with a brown filter before he spoke.

"An alibi? Not one that you'd believe," he announced with a smirk.

"Did anyone see you that night?" Harper prodded.

Ridley shook his head.

"We were all busy," Lucky said. "Didn't know we'd need to keep track of each other for alibis."

"Did any of you see him at all? Walking around here? Something?"

Lucky and Jimmy exchanged glances but neither of them spoke.

"Covering for him doesn't do any of you any favors. Especially if you're next on his list."

That got Grace's attention and her head shot up.

"Ma'am, did you see Ridley that night?"

She shook her head. "After dinner, he usually just goes to his trailer. I didn't see him, but I wasn't exactly looking for him either."

"What about you?" Harper nodded at Jimmy.

"Uh, well, you see, sir…" Jimmy looked like a deer caught in headlights. "I'm blind as a bat without my glasses. Lost them the last town we visited and as you can imagine, it's hard to replace them when you're with a traveling circus. So, I might've seen him, but I can't say for sure."

"You?" He looked down at Lucky.

"Nope. Can't say I did."

"I saw him." Coralee spoke up. I hadn't heard her approach.

I glanced at Ridley to gauge his reaction but he remained stoic.

"Ridley, I saw you out walking that night. You went right past my tent."

"Why didn't you tell us this before?" Harper asked.

Coralee shrugged. "I mentioned it to that officer the other night. The big guy. That girl was with him." She motioned to me. "Remember?" She raised her eyebrows at me. "I told you both that I saw him walk past my tent the night Chuckles died. Straight off of the circus grounds."

I shook my head. "No, you didn't."

"I'm sure I did," she said firmly.

Harper looked at me expectantly.

Curly stepped forward and pulled at Harper's arm. "Ridley didn't kill Chuckles. They were friends. Me and Chuckles and Ridley were best friends. Right, Ridley?" Curly looked up at Ridley, his eyes pleading and for the first time I saw Ridley soften.

"That's right, buddy," he said quietly.

"Wait," I said, my eyes searching the ground as I replayed events over in my mind.

"I think it'll be for the best if we get this sorted out down at the station," Harper was saying.

"Wait," I said again, the pieces coming together in my mind like seeing the final moves needed to solve a rubix cube. Actually, I'd never solved one myself, but I imagine that's what it would feel like.

Harper was grabbing Ridley under the arm while Curly protested loudly.

"Did you and Elsa plan this together?" Coralee was saying.

"Wait!" I shouted this time. Harper froze and eight pairs of expectant eyes stared back at me.

"I know who did it," I said. "I know who killed them."

CHAPTER 15

"The first day we met Elsa, you asked her if she was an acrobat and she said she was terrified of heights. Whoever set Ferdinand up to die would had to have not only climbed all the way up to the top platform, but they would've had to put themselves in a fairly dangerous situation in order to tamper with the trapeze. It must've been someone comfortable with doing that on a regular basis."

"That night after it happened, I was sneaking around outside the tent and I saw you and Jimmy talking. He was pointing up to the trapeze and said he could see that the mechanism had been tampered with. Now, at the time I thought it was an odd angle for you two to be standing at for him to see it, even with great vision, but I brushed it off."

Turning to Jimmy, I delivered the final blow. "You just said you're blind as a bat without your glasses. How could you have seen what was wrong with the trapeze then? You couldn't have —unless you already knew."

Jimmy's eyes widened.

"What are you saying?" Harper asked.

"I'm saying that if Jimmy didn't do it, then he knew about it. Meaning he knows who did. Earlier, the three of you were telling me that you shared your suspicions about Elsa with the police. You wanted me to think she killed Ferdinand and Chuckles."

"What are you getting at?" Grace snarled.

"I think you set Elsa up. And I don't think Chuckles' murder had anything to do with my store being broken into. I think Chuckles saw you and was walking to the police station. You just happened to catch up with him right outside my building and murdered him there."

I turned back to Ridley. "I know you're the one who broke into my place and I know why. But you *really* didn't see anything happen? Chuckles was your friend. Why would you cover for his killer?"

For the first time, Ridley looked defeated. He lowered his head. "I really didn't see who killed him," he whispered. "I didn't even know he was out there. I didn't hear anything because I was playing my harmonica." His eyes met mine then. "To make sure whoever was in your building wouldn't wake up. When I left, I saw him lying there." He shook his head. "I checked for a pulse... but he was gone. There was nothing I could do to help him at that point and I was only going to risk getting myself caught if I called the police. So I just—ran."

"So, Jimmy, care to shed some light?" Harper asked.

"I, uh..." Jimmy stuttered. "Look, it wasn't my idea."

Lucky smacked him hard in the stomach. "Idiot!" He spat. "Always running your mouth and having to tell people about your problems." He leered. "Oh, I can't see," he said in a singsong tone, clearly mocking Jimmy.

"I'm sorry, Lucky!" Jimmy said frantically.

"You didn't have to out us too!" Lucky motioned between him and Grace.

"He didn't, stupid! But *you* just did!" Grace hit Lucky in the back of the head.

He yelped and rubbed at the spot.

"It was just supposed to be Ferdinand," Jimmy started, holding his hands up defensively. "Just to frame Elsa or Marvin."

"Elsa *or* Marvin?"

"Either one. Really didn't matter," Jimmy continued. "If we could get rid of one of 'em, then it'd be easier to push the other out."

"Why kill Marvin then?" I asked.

"That was Lucky's idea." Grace piped up.

"You boneheads weren't arresting her. We left you clues and handed you a suspect on a silver platter and still ya kept poking around here like bumbling idiots. We had to do something! Besides, Marvin deserved it, the way he was using Coralee." Lucky looked over at her.

She gave him a confused look in return.

"Figured using one of Elsa's knives to kill her cheating lover would be the most obvious thing left to do."

"Why not just do that first then? Or just kill Elsa if you hated her so much?"

"Because we all had a strained relationship with both of them. It would've put suspicion on us. But Ferdinand, we all got along with him. Elsa and Marvin didn't though, see. So it was the perfect plan, really."

"Well, I think we've heard enough." Harper gave Dobson a look and Dobson spoke into his radio for backup.

Jimmy and Grace both gave each other a look and before I knew it, they had taken off. Lucky stood frozen for a moment before shouting, "I love you, Coralee! I always will!" and then scampered off behind them.

"What a bunch of chickens," I muttered.

It took a few seconds longer than it had before, but the blue smoke began to form around each of them. Then the squawking started.

"Well, this ought to be interesting," Granny said.

Ironically, Lucky was the largest chicken. A great big brown thing that worked himself into such a frenzy that he ran straight into a bright yellow pole, knocking himself out. Jimmy and Grace were smaller in size, and both a plain cream color.

"Dru," Harper said defeated. "Come on, Dobson."

Dobson had an incredulous look on his face but all he said was, "Chicken herding is not in my job description."

"It is today, my friend." Harper smiled before shifting into a fox.

Dobson attempted words, but his mouth only moved.

Granny laughed next to me. "That one probably needs a memory spell later. I'm not sure he can handle this information."

"And I can easily perform one once I have my ring back." I turned back to Ridley who was eyeing me carefully.

"Come on. Give it up." I held my hand out. "Don't make me turn you into something too. I don't know what it will be though, so I wouldn't take my chances if I were you."

He stuck his hand in his pocket and pulled it out, hesitating for a moment.

"I *am* sorry I stole it," he said before placing it in my palm.

"Yeah, you have some explaining to do."

"Do I?"

I nodded. "Explaining why you stole my ring, how you

know who I am, and what the heck that cage is all about in your trailer."

"So you *were* in my trailer?" He gave me a half smile.

"Come on. Spill it."

He sighed. "Fine. I guess I'll start at the beginning then."

"That's usually the best place to start."

"As you've already figured out, I'm a light wizard."

"No, light wizards are good." Granny said sternly.

"*A* light wizard?" I questioned him.

"Well, I mean, it might depend on who you ask." He shrugged one shoulder. "I used to be a dark wizard, or a warlock. I practiced dark magic. but I've changed. I'm good now. I really am," he said. "I'm also known as a bard. So I have to use music to control my magic. When I first came into my magic, I was mentored by someone. He would tell me stories about the family he used to have. The most powerful witches in the world. Women with snow white hair with a touch of crimson. And a ring that they owned. He told me they lived here in Blackwood Bay and owned a building right in the middle of town. When I heard we were coming here, it was like fate had dropped this gift in my lap. I thought if I could get your ring, then I could use its magic to break this curse."

"What curse?"

"The witch that gave me her magic… when I was young, only eighteen years old, I met a witch. She told me I could have unlimited power, and she offered to give it to me because she was a good person and I needed it more than she did. I was naive and enamored with her and once I agreed, there was no going back. What she didn't tell me was that it came with a terrible curse. At night, I turn into a beast."

"Sorry?"

"That's why I have the cage. I lock myself in and it keeps the rest of the world safe. I haven't met anyone powerful enough to break it, and I thought maybe I could use your ring and do it myself. It didn't work though."

"The ring only works for its rightful owner. Why didn't you just ask?"

He gave me a confused look.

"Why didn't you just come ask me if I could help you?"

"Well, that's... I didn't actually think of that," he said, scratching the back of his head as the realization continued dawning on him. "I've spent so long keeping my identity and my curse a secret. I haven't met many people like me. I guess the thought never occurred to me."

"I can try. If you like."

His eyes lit up. "Really? Even after I broke into your building and stole from you?"

A chicken zoomed in between us and Dobson stumbled behind it. Harper sauntered up, Lucky tucked up under his arm. "Aw, come on, Dobson, you act like you've never wrangled Gloria Powders' chickens before." He heckled.

"Maybe I can help," Ridley offered, pulling his harmonica from his pocket.

"Wait!" Harper and I both shouted.

"You don't trust me?" He acted offended.

"Not as far as I can throw you," I said.

"Here." He stuffed his hand in his inner coat pocket and dug around for a few moments before pulling out a handful of individually packaged earplugs. He held them out to me and Harper with a smile.

"You just carry these around?"

He shrugged. "Never know when you might need them."

Harper set Lucky down and we both put the neon-colored earplugs in our ears. Ridley brought the harmonica to his lips and in a matter of seconds, the chickens froze, turning their heads eerily in Ridley's direction. They moved slowly, forming a single line and he began to walk backward leading them toward the exit.

I had been too busy observing the chickens' behavior to notice Dobson until he passed by, holding up the rear and obviously under Ridley's spell as well. Harper and Granny and I followed him in awe as he led them all out the exit. He motioned to Harper's car. Harper nodded and raced to the back door of his cruiser. He opened it and all three chickens hopped in, followed by Dobson. As soon as he shut the door, Ridley pulled the harmonica from his lips and placed it carefully back in his pocket.

I pulled the earplugs from my ears. "You *are* the gosh-darn pied piper!"

"I owed you," he said before turning to Harper. "Should wear off in about a half hour or so."

"Wait. The chickens..." I searched Ridley's face for some hint of recognition.

He gave me a sheepish grin and rubbed the back of his neck with one hand, "Like I said, you lied to me. I don't like when people lie to me."

"So you punished me by setting chickens loose in my bookstore?"

He scrunched up his face and shrugged, "I *am* sorry."

"You know, you're not exactly the poster boy for morality yourself. Breaking and entering and stealing things that don't belong to you."

He stuffed his hands in his pockets and leaned back on his heels. "Well, you've got me there."

"Thanks again!" Harper called out and gave Ridley a slight nod before climbing into his cruiser. I was hoping he'd acknowledge me so I could give him the apology he deserved, but maybe now wasn't the best time anyway. I watched him pull away and tried to ignore the knot forming in my stomach.

When I turned back around, Ridley was already making his way back, a small figure in black between brightly colored tents. I had no idea what kind of curse had been put on Ridley or how powerful it was. I'd never tried to break a curse before, either.

I turned around and continued to make my way home.

"Weird day," I said aloud.

"That's an understatement," Granny replied.

After that, the silence hung heavy in the air between us as my mind continued to race.

CHAPTER 16

I walked in at some point during the middle of Dorothy reading Tilly and Eve the riot act for letting me go to the circus alone earlier. Minnie stood idly next to her sister, visibly upset as her eyes darted back and forth.

I attempted to intervene, but there was no stopping her on the warpath today. I plopped myself down on the barstool behind the counter and pulled Maui into my lap. He was dressed in his shiny black fur coat again and I was hoping that meant he was no longer upset with me.

"Can you die from a conversation?" he asked. "Because she's been babbling on for over an hour now and it feels like you could die from it."

I gave a little laugh.

"What's wrong with you? Granny said you caught the killers." He snuggled into my lap a little deeper and nuzzled his face against my hand.

"We did. It's just… I was a jerk to Harper."

"Mmm… first lovers' quarrel," he teased.

"I owe him an apology…" I absentmindedly stroked his ear.

"So what are you waiting for?"

"He took the suspects in. He's probably really busy."

"You could at least call and leave a message. Then he can get ahold of you when he's free," Mom suggested.

"I should apologize in person though. It's always hard to show how sincere you are over the phone, especially when you goofed as bad as I did earlier."

I glanced at the clock on the wall. It had been at least an hour since I'd arrived back at the store. Maybe he had a little free time to chat by now.

"I'll just call the station and see if he's busy first. Then I can run down there and give him a decent apology."

I found the Blackwood Bay Police Department number with my phone and Jolene answered in two rings. She was as much of a staple at the small police station as Chief Carver was and she'd been there just as long. She also knew about us witches. I hadn't heard the full story yet, but it had something to do with a nasty ex and our coven coming to the rescue and serving up some vigilante justice.

"Blackwood Bay Police Department. This is Jolene." She said in her usual chipper tone.

"Hi Jolene. It's Dru Davis. Is Sergeant Harper busy?" I asked.

"Oh hi, sweetie," she said. "They released that circus woman and Harper offered to drive her back down there, so he's not in at the moment."

"How long ago did they leave?"

"Oh, you just missed him. Do you want me to take a message?"

"No thanks, Jolene. I'll catch up with him later." I hung up and glanced down at my phone screen for a few moments longer. "He's taking Elsa back to the circus," I said to Mom and Maui.

I called his cell phone next but it went to voicemail. I considered that maybe it was intentional, but dismissed the thought quickly. Weighing my options for a moment, I sat there bouncing my leg.

"Jeez, woman. You're going to give me motion sickness," Maui complained.

I lifted him from my lap and placed him carefully on the barstool.

"You're leaving again so soon?" he said.

"Yes. I have to talk to him."

"Why don't you just call him and ask him to stop by when he's done?" Maui, always the logical one.

"I did call him. And he didn't answer. Maybe on purpose." I idly chewed at the end of my thumbnail. "I'm going," I said impulsively as I walked around the front of the counter.

"Where are you going?" Dorothy paused her tirade.

"Back to the circus."

"Why?" Her and Granny said in unison.

"I need to talk to Harper. He's on his way back to drop off Elsa. And I need to hurry if I'm going to catch him."

"But the bard—" Dorothy started.

"He's not a threat." I cut her off. "He's harmless."

"Maybe that's just what he wants you to think." She raised her eyebrows at me. "Do you want me to come along?" She gave a pointed look at Tilly and Eve.

I thought for a moment. "To listen to my private conversation with Harper? No." I felt a smile spreading across my face. "But I do have something else I might need your help with."

"Is it dangerous?" Minnie asked.

"Oh, *very*." I waggled my eyebrows up and down, trying to

get the sarcasm across loud and clear, but no one in the room seemed to notice.

"Maybe we should all go," Tilly said.

"No, no. We don't need the whole posse. Besides, Tilly, I need you to visit the police station." I said.

"Memory spell?" She asked.

"Please," I nodded, "Chief Carver will fill you in on the details."

"So it's just us then?" Dorothy asked expectantly.

"Granny's coming too."

"I am?" She looked up from the magazine she was peering at and I gave her my sweetest smile.

"Oh, be careful, girls!" Minnie clutched Dorothy's arm.

"Yes, we will be," Dorothy said resolutely.

"I love you both," Minnie said.

"I love you too," Dorothy assured her.

We made our way out of the bookstore and I turned to the right.

"Walking or driving?" Dorothy asked.

"Oh, I hadn't considered that we even had an option since I don't have a car yet. Did you drive over?" I asked.

"Yes, but I just told my sister that I love her. I'm obviously in no condition to drive," she said.

I snickered, "Walking it is then."

I filled Dorothy in on the day's events and I had just finished up when we saw the circus come into view. Harper's cruiser was parked on the side of the street but it was empty.

"Well, he's here. Maybe he walked her inside?" I said.

I noticed the crew members had already started cleaning up the place and tearing down the setup even though it was already almost dusk. We followed the dirt pathway around to the row of trailers. The tent that they'd used to cover their common eating area was still up and I spotted Coralee sitting alone and watching us as we walked past. I heard voices up ahead and instantly recognized Harper's. He stepped out from between two trailers, Curly next to him.

Curly noticed us first and raised his arm in a friendly wave.

"Hi, Curly," I said as we approached.

"Thank you for helping my mom." He beamed. "And Ridley too. I knew neither one of them did it."

"You're welcome." I said. "Would you excuse us for a moment?" I asked, motioning to Harper.

"Sure thing." Curly gave a slight nod.

"Can I talk with you?" I looked at Harper, the bruise on his eye was really obvious now.

He nodded and put a light hand on my back, and we walked just far enough to be out of earshot of anyone else.

"I'm so sorry," I blurted out. "I acted like an immature, ungrateful little… well, you know. I shouldn't have treated you that way. I feel really terrible about it. And I'm really sorry about your eye too."

He cocked his head to the side and stared at me for a moment. "All right," he finally said.

"All right?"

"Yeah, all right." A grin tugged at the corner of his mouth. "I forgive you."

"Just like that?"

"Just like that." He paused. "Look, Dru, I know this is all new for you. It's all new for me too, you know. We're still figuring out how to do this dance. You and me. Sometimes you'll step on my toes and sometimes I'll step on yours. But acknowledging that and apologizing goes a long way."

I let out a sigh of relief. "That's a really good analogy for it. Thank you for being so understanding."

"I'm sorry too. For making you feel like, I don't know…
like I didn't want you around or that I didn't think your theories
were any good. I just wanted to keep you safe. That's all," he
said.

"I know."

"You have to say you forgive me." He winked.

"I forgive you." I laughed.

"What did you come all the way back here for anyway?"

"To find you and apologize."

"Really?" He seemed surprised.

"Yes, really." I shifted my weight nervously onto my left
foot and fidgeted with my ring, glad to finally have it back on
my finger. "So how did it go? How's Dobson?"

Harper chuckled. "He's probably going to need a little help,
if you know what I mean."

"I'll have Tilly come by the station later and work her magic
on him."

"I hope you're referring to a memory spell." He joked.
"Chief Carver and him were still working on those three when I
left though."

"What do you mean?"

"Well, they were all singing like canaries when it came to
Ferdinand's death, and Lucky admitted to acting alone when it
came to murdering Marvin, but none of them will fess up to
what happened to Chuckles."

"That's odd, don't you think?" I crinkled my nose. "I mean,
Chuckles was killed because he probably saw something he
wasn't supposed to, right?"

"Yeah, that's the theory." He shrugged. "We don't have any
evidence to tie them to that specific crime though. But at least
they'll go down for the other two."

"What about the cigarette butt?" I asked.

"Still at the lab. It's only been a couple days."

"I know, but did you ever figure out if it belonged to Chuckles?"

"Well, he didn't have any on him and the pack we found in his trailer was different, but that doesn't mean it didn't belong to him."

I nodded. "That's true. But did you check the other performers? I saw Jimmy and Grace both smoking earlier today."

"Yeah, we checked. No luck."

"Hmm…" I twisted my ring around my finger.

"What?"

"I don't know. It's just strange. That's all."

"Didn't you ever work a case where you still had unanswered questions, even after you'd solved it?" He asked.

"Yeah, of course. There's—" I shook my head. "You're right. Listen, there's something else I was thinking about too. And I might need your help."

"Sure," he said.

I walked past him, lightly touching his arm as I did, and headed straight for Curly again.

"Do you know where Ridley is?" I asked Curly.

"He just went to his trailer." He looked from me to Harper. "Is everything all right?"

"Yes, everything's fine. There's just something I wanted to try to help him with."

"Oh, you mean his nocturnal problem?" Curly asked.

"How did you know about that?"

"I told you, we're friends. I'm the one who keeps the extra set of keys for the locks. Check in on him every now and again too."

"You're a good friend," Harper said.

"Can you really help him? Are you able to do magic too?" His eyes widened.

I knelt down and lowered my voice. "Yes, I am. And I really hope I can help your friend. Do you want to come with us?"

He nodded.

"Let's go then." I motioned for Curly to lead the way and we followed him back to Ridley's trailer.

He moved aside and I stepped forward and gave a solid rap on the door. A moment later, it swung open.

"Ah, you're back." He gave me a half smile.

"Yes." Can we come in?"

"All of you?" He asked. "It'll be a tight squeeze, but sure." He stepped inside and allowed us all to pile into his tiny trailer.

I barely waited for Dorothy to shut the door before I spoke. "Tell me about this man who mentored you. He said I was his family?" I asked.

"Nope. That's not what we're here for," Granny said firmly.

I held a hand up to quiet her. Not that that ever worked.

Ridley nodded. "Lucian Mandrake. He said was your grandfather."

Granny spit at his name. Again.

"Oh, heavens!" Dorothy brought her hand to her chest and took a dramatic step back.

"He was my mentor for many years. He was the one who taught me bard magic."

"Are you still in contact with him?" I asked.

He shook his head. "No, we had a falling out, one might call it."

"About what?"

"I don't mind using my magic for certain types of nefarious activities, as you're well aware, but I don't want to be decidedly wicked either. I didn't want to be a dark wizard anymore. Lucian didn't take that too well."

"So you're telling me my grandfather is… what? Like, an evil old wizard?" I felt my eyes widen as the realization sank in.

Ridley gave me a sympathetic look. "I'm afraid so."

"Guess nothing's changed then," Granny said under her breath.

"Wow." That was all I could manage.

"Oh, Dru." Dorothy let out a sympathetic sigh.

"Sorry to be the one to tell you. I figured you already knew."

"No, it's all right. I should've known," I said, shooting a look in both Granny and Dorothy's direction.

"Why? What's the point?" Granny muttered.

"Thanks, Ridley."

"You're welcome." He smiled. "Is your grandmother still around?"

"Uh, well, sort of. She died recently but her spirit is with us. She's here now, in fact."

"You can see her?" He seemed shocked.

"Yes."

"Can she hear us?"

I nodded.

He cleared his throat and spoke in a voice louder than necessary. "Hello, Drusilla. Uh, Ms. Rathmore. My name is Herbert Ridley."

"Your name is Herbert?" I interjected.

"It's not like we get to choose. It's why I go by Ridley." He raised his chin and spoke into the room again. "I just thought you should know… uh, I just thought you should know that Lucian, he never spoke an ill word about you. He had an immense amount of love and respect for you. And your daughter." He paused, uncertain, and looked back at me. "Did she hear me?"

I glanced at Granny, who stood with her arms wrapped tightly around her and a scowl on her face. Her eyes met mine but she didn't say anything.

"She did. Thanks, Ridley. Now tell me more about this curse," I said.

"Well," he let out a deep exhale, "all I know is that it came with my magic. From the witch who gave it to me. In order to get rid of it, I'd have to gift it to someone else. The magic and the curse. And I'm just not willing to do that. So, every night, at exactly 3 a.m., I turn into a disgusting beast. And I stay that way until the sun comes up. When there's a full moon, it lasts from sundown until sunup. I've gotten in the habit of locking myself up every night in that cage over there. Curly keeps a spare key for me just in case and checks on me in the mornings."

Curly gave a nod. "I saw him once. The beast. Real scary. Kinda like a... a werewolf and a bird had a baby." He looked up like he was thinking, "And then stuck a horn on its head too."

"The transition is excruciating." Ridley added.

"There has to be a way to reverse it," I said, tapping my chin with my forefinger.

"The witch said that there wasn't. That's why she was willing to give her magic away. It was the only way to rid herself of it," Ridley said.

"Maybe *she* couldn't reverse it, but that doesn't mean I can't."

CHAPTER 17

"This isn't going to work, Dru," Granny was saying, though I could barely hear her over the sound of Dorothy lecturing Ridley about how lucky he was that I was here to help him and not have Harper throw his butt in jail for breaking in and stealing from me.

"You're just not strong enough yet. You've only had your magic for a month! And this isn't just some silly little curse. There was a witch—an experienced witch—who was willing to give everything up to get rid of it because it was too powerful to break."

"Can everyone please be quiet!?" I barked. My head had started to pound and I rubbed my temples. "Ridley, sit." I motioned to the pullout couch and he hurried to comply.

"Dorothy, give me your hand." I held one hand out to her and wrapped hers tightly in mine. "Curly, Harper, and Granny," I said, giving her a pointed look, "I need you all to be very quiet so I can concentrate."

Curly and Harper nodded and Granny gave me a pout.

"Thank you," I said. "Ridley, I don't know if this will work. I don't even know how we'll know if it did. But I'm willing to try."

"I appreciate it." He let out a deep breath.

I closed my eyes and focused on centering my magic in my chest the way Granny had taught me. I could feel my ring getting warm on my finger so I figured that meant something was working.

I probably should've consulted the spell book, I thought. *Or at least asked Granny if she knew like a chant or something I was supposed to do.* I was a rookie and I hadn't thought this through very well. *Guess I'll just wing it.*

Gripping Dorothy's hand tighter, I could feel heat radiating from it in waves. I started to think I'd need to pull my hand away as the heat intensified, but then I realized it was moving up to my wrist. As I focused on it, I realized *I* was the one moving it.

It was a little difficult at first, but I managed to transfer it up my arm and across my shoulder until it settled itself in the center of my chest. I felt a cold sweat break out on my forehead and the heaviness in my chest was making it hard to breathe. I worked hard to concentrate on what I wanted, just like Granny had shown me.

In the movies, they always have like a cute little rhyming spell they chant. Granted, this wasn't the movies, but that was the only source of knowledge I had to tap into at the moment.

"Reverse the curse," I whispered under my breath. My magic, up until that moment, had felt like an elephant sitting on my chest. Suddenly, I felt a jolt all over my body and it jerked me forward. Instinctively, I opened my eyes and held out my hand to steady myself. My amber ring was glowing, its various shades swirling around each other. I caught Ridley's pained expression behind it.

"Are you okay?" I choked out, feeling Harper's hand come around my waist to help steady me.

Dorothy dropped my other hand and set to work wiping my forehead with a towel that had come from somewhere.

Ridley stood, and glanced at Dorothy and Harper. "Did you see that?" he asked.

"See what?" My voice was shaky.

"That burst of light that came out of you." His eyes were wide.

"Did it hurt you?" I asked, remembering the pained expression on his face.

He shook his head. "Not exactly." He began pulling his suit jacket off and unbuttoning his white dress shirt with trembling fingers.

"What are you doing?" Harper asked, a suspicious look on his face.

"There's a mark." He grunted as he pulled his shirt from his pants and yanked it off over his head. He threw it on the floor and looked down at the spot on his chest just between his pectoral and shoulder muscles. "Oh my God," he whispered, running his fingers across his smooth skin and then looking back up at me.

"There—there was a mark here—more like a tattoo. Some weird symbol that appeared after I received the curse. Look! It's gone!" He looked back up at me, his eyes dancing. A huge smile spread across his face and before I knew it, he had me wrapped in his arms and lifted off the ground. "You did it!" He shouted in my ear. "You really did it!"

He spun me around and I caught a glimpse of Curly jumping up and down excitedly, and Harper and Dorothy smiling. For the first time, I spotted Granny standing in the corner, a bewildered look on her face.

"I'm so proud of you!" Dorothy shouted over Ridley's excited cries. She had a smile on her face and tears rimming her eyes, and I knew she really meant it.

I looked back to gauge Granny's reaction, but she was gone.

CHAPTER 18

"Oh, I wish the girls could've been here to see you!" Dorothy was gushing as we left Ridley's trailer. "Wolf," She addressed Harper by his first name and waited for him to look at her before she spoke, "do you have any idea how amazing that was? She shouldn't have been able to do it, but she did." She beamed and held me at arms' length.

"Our girl is pretty special." Harper turned his head to look at me.

"Stop, you two," I said, though I probably didn't mean it.

"Should we get out of here?" Harper asked.

"Yes, it's been a long day." I started walking back toward the exit, flanked on either side by Harper and Dorothy. I spotted Coralee still planted in the same spot and staring at us as we passed. I hesitated.

"Just a minute." I said, before hurrying over to her. I plopped down on the bench across from her, deciding to go for the direct approach. "I need to ask you something."

She looked a little surprised at first, but she composed

herself and folded her hands on the weathered wooden table between us. "Go ahead."

"Why did you lie to us? To me?"

"I'm not sure what you're referring to." She studied her hands, refusing to make eye contact.

"You said you saw Ferdinand fall, but I know that was a lie. And then you said that you told me and that cop, Dobson, that you saw Ridley that night. But that was a lie too. Who knows what else you lied about? The question is why."

She sucked in a deep breath and closed her eyes while she exhaled. "When Ferdinand died, I wasn't in the tent. I never was during that act. It was when Marvin and I would have our little secret rendezvous. Everyone would be in the big top watching or performing and he only needed to be there to introduce the acts. The acrobats had the longest performance so, naturally that's when we snuck away. Except that night, he never came. I waited in my tent and some kids came in for a reading so I was stuck and unable to go see what had held him up. And then Ferdinand was killed."

"Why didn't you just tell us you were giving a reading? We wouldn't have thought twice about it."

"Because I wasn't supposed to be there. I was *supposed* to be in the big top. I was afraid if the other performers found out, they'd start asking questions and Marvin and I would be found out. So, I lied." She continued to study her hands, refusing to make eye contact.

"And what about Ridley?"

"I really did see him that night. Out walking. I didn't think much of it at the time, and Ridley, he's weird but harmless. So I never told anyone I saw him the night Chuckles died. But once I thought he was the one that killed Marvin, well, that's when I decided to tell the truth."

I weighed her words carefully and something told me she was telling the truth. I reached out and placed my hand over hers, "Thanks, Coralee. Are you going to be okay?"

She shrugged. "Marvin is gone, I just lost five other allies... Elsa, she won't let me stay."

"You don't know that." I tried to sound reassuring.

"*I* do." That familiar German accent came from behind me and I turned to see Elsa approaching. I spotted Harper and Dorothy making their way toward us too.

Elsa wore a long silky black robe over matching pajamas and a pair of black peep toe heels with a strip of fur across the top. Her hair was still pinned back, but she'd washed the makeup from her face.

"Hi, Elsa. It's nice to see you again. Are you doing all right?" I asked apprehensively.

"Am I doing all right?" She erupted in a short burst of laughter. "Oh, dear." She reached out and patted me on the arm. "My ex-husband was murdered, my lover was murdered, and my performers set me up to take the fall for it." She laughed again. "The imbeciles really thought they'd get away with it." She shook her head.

I glanced at Coralee who still had her head hung low. "And Chuckles," she mumbled.

"What?" Elsa still had a smile on her face, but her eyes shot daggers at Coralee. "Beg your pardon, homewrecker? What are you still doing here anyway?" She spat.

"Maybe you should calm down." Dorothy put a hand on Elsa's shoulder.

"I will once I don't have to look at her face anymore!" Her eyes seemed to grow wilder by the second.

Coralee hunched her back and sank down further. "I'll be gone by morning," she said in a shaky voice.

Having been betrayed by my fiancé and best friend just a few months before, I could easily empathize with Elsa and the range of emotions she was experiencing. I know I certainly settled on rage for a while. But Coralee seemed so weak sitting there getting her butt handed to her, I couldn't help but feel a little sorry for her.

"Why don't you head back to your tent?" Harper addressed Coralee. "I'll have Dobson come by and we'll help you work out a plan. How does that sound?"

Coralee stood, her hands shaking and cheeks tear-stained. "Thank you," she whispered and kept her head low as she hurried away.

"That's *my* tent, you know?" Elsa said to Harper, fishing around in her pocket.

"Yes, ma'am." He nodded.

"I'm sorry you all had to witness my outbursts today." She sighed and looked at each of us for a moment. "It's been a terrible, terrible past few days."

"Of course, dear. We understand." Dorothy gave her forearm a sympathetic squeeze. I had turned completely on the bench, but with Elsa and Dorothy standing so close to me, I didn't have much space to stand up. I decided to stay seated, the hard wooden bench already making my backside sore. I scanned the empty field for Granny, confused as to why she'd disappeared so suddenly. *Is she mad at me for trying to help Ridley? Is she mad at me because it actually worked?*

And that's when I saw him. The moment I'd been anticipating since my first chance encounter with his lifeless body outside my building. The one and only Chuckles the clown.

CHAPTER 19

The sun had almost gone down completely, but his white and red suit seemed to almost glow in the night. It looked like he was moving closer and I could make out his white face paint and red wig. I wanted to scream, but no sound came out when I opened my mouth. He was coming closer, his gait stiff and his gaze fixated on me. I felt my hands dampen with sweat and a cold chill ran up my spine.

This was it. He was coming for me. I squeezed my eyes shut tight, hoping he wouldn't be there when I opened them and wondered if ghosts were able to hurt people. I mentally kicked myself for never having asked that question before. I opened my eyes and saw him still making his way toward me and decided that I needed to try really hard to scream again. That's when I saw motion next to him. It was harder to make out in the darkness, but as they neared, I realized it was Trixie walking with him. Trixie, in her cute little cat sweater and plaid skirt, her pigtails bouncing at the back of her head as she walked. Trixie was a twenty-something who had worked for Granny before I'd come to Blackwood Bay and she'd been murdered by the same person who had killed Granny. She was my first ghostly encounter and she still came back to visit me often.

She threw her arm up in a friendly wave and looped her other arm through Chuckles'. I felt the pit in my stomach start to dissipate. If Trixie had made friends with him, then I knew I didn't have anything to fear. Trixie would have been a few cards short of a full deck, but I knew she would never let anything bad happen to me. I watched Chuckles closely and though he might've looked terrifying, he was just a man after all. A man who had been murdered by someone close to him. I couldn't help but feel pity for him.

Elsa and Dorothy were chattering on about something, but I stood and brushed past them to meet Trixie and Chuckles. I gave Harper a slight nod to come with me, so I didn't look like I was standing in the middle of an empty field talking to myself.

"Hi, Trixie," I greeted her.

"Trixie's here?" Harper asked.

"With Chuckles."

He raised his eyebrows at me.

"Dru! Hiya! This is my friend." She hugged Chuckles' arm. "His name is Chuckles." She giggled. "He was scared to come talk to you, but I told him we were friends and that you were a nice lady who could help him." She nodded her head enthusiastically.

"That's right, Trixie." I offered a kind smile, "Hi, Chuckles."

He kept his head down but looked up at me.

"Uh, could you not look at me like that?" I asked, motioning for him to lift his head up. "It's really creepy."

"Sorry." He promptly lifted his chin and glanced at Trixie.

"It's okay." She rubbed his arm, encouragingly.

"You don't like clowns?" he asked. I'm not sure what I expected, but he had a regular man's voice. Nothing out of the ordinary or sinister about it at all.

"Don't take it personally," I said. "You know, we've been looking for you. Well, I have. I'm the only one here who can see you other than Trixie."

"That's what Trixie said." He looked over at Trixie for reassurance and shifted his feet nervously.

"Chuckles was scared to come back here." Trixie explained.

"Why were you scared to come back, Chuckles?" I asked in a way that would bring Harper into the loop on what was being said.

"I was murdered, remember?" His eyes darted around nervously.

"I know that. But you're a ghost now. No one can hurt you. No one can even *see* you. Besides, they arrested the people that hurt you today. You don't ever have to see them again."

"What people?" He shook his head, "It wasn't people. Just one person."

"Well, sure. I mean they arrested Lucky, Jimmy, and Grace. But maybe you can tell us exactly which one did it."

"No!" He shook his head forcefully, "No, it wasn't any of them. It's still not safe here." He started looking around frantically, his eyes darting left to right and back again a few times.

"Please calm down." I held my hands up.

"What's going on?" Harper asked.

"He says it wasn't them."

Chuckles widened his eyes and in an instant, he was gone.

I gasped. "No."

"Aw, shoot! It took so much work to get him here." Trixie stuck out her lower lip in a pout.

"How did you know we needed to talk to him?" I asked.

"Oh, I didn't really. I found him wandering around down at the beach and we started talking. I told him we had to find you so you could help him just like you helped me." A smile replaced the scowl on the face.

"Do you think he might've gone back there? To the beach?" I asked.

"He said he likes it down there." She nodded.

"Okay, can you see if you can find him again? Tell him we won't let anything bad happen to him, but we need to know who killed him and it doesn't look like we're going to figure it out without his help," I explained.

Trixie had her face scrunched up in confusion.

"Find Chuckles. Tell him I'm a witch and I'll keep him safe. Bring him back. Got it?"

She nodded, her pigtails bobbing up and down. She gave a quick wave before disappearing into the night air.

"Great." I sighed, turning back to Harper.

"So he said it wasn't Jimmy, Lucky, or Grace?" he asked.

"That's what he said." I crossed my arms.

We started back toward Dorothy and Elsa, sitting at the picnic table now and giggling like old friends, the aroma of cigarette smoke wafting through the air.

"Everything all right?" Elsa looked up as we approached, a wide smile still spread on her face after a fit of laughter.

Harper nodded.

"Thank you again for clearing my name." She pointed her cigarette at me and I noticed she didn't have her fancy vintage holder this evening. "I'm so sorry for bringing this mess to your town. And into your home." She brought her hand down and hovered it above an old green glass ashtray. "I don't know what that Ridley was after, but I do hope you got it back." She placed her thumb on the end of the filter, just below the purple band and gave it a little flick, a bit of ash falling from the tip.

"Is that the lucky one?" I asked, feeling my pulse quicken.

She glanced down at the cigarette in her hand and back up at me.

"The joker." I said evenly.

Harper widened his stance next to me and I knew he understood.

She twisted it gently between her fingers and showed me the joker emblem, a half smile forming on her face. "My papa smoked these. When I was a little girl, I used to steal the jokers because I knew they were the lucky ones. I'd keep them in a box under my bed. He never said a word about it." She got a far off look in her eyes. "Nowadays, I just keep these and throw away the rest of the pack."

"You know that's the cigarette brand we found next to Chuckles body," Harper said.

"Why, that's an uncanny coincidence, isn't it?" She brought the cigarette to her lips and took a long drag from it.

"I highly doubt that," Harper responded. "We'll have the DNA from it soon."

"Well, be sure to call and let me know what you find. We'll be long gone, I'm sure."

"You know what else is an uncanny coincidence?" I said. "No one knew Ridley was the one that broke into my building."

"Pardon?" She furrowed her brow.

"Yeah, no one knew. It wasn't information that was shared." Harper backed me up.

"He told Curly, my son. They're the best of friends," she explained, waving a dismissive hand.

"How would he have had time to do that though? Harper has been with either you or Ridley since you were released today."

"I don't know. Maybe he told me yesterday. Semantics."
She stubbed out her cigarette in the ashtray and stood. "You're
barking up the wrong tree." She pointed an accusing finger.

"You're right. Whoever killed Chuckles and framed the
others, man, that was a smart play," Harper said.

"Definitely," I agreed. "I mean, that takes a certain level of
cunningness that would be hard to pull off."

"Who is smart enough though?" Dorothy decided to chime
in. "Maybe that Marvin fellow did it."

"Marvin?" Elsa laughed. "Please. He was a moron too.
They're all morons. Every last one of them. Thinking they
could frame me and not get caught? Ha! As if they could really
pull that off."

"So that's why you killed Chuckles then." I said. "You're
smarter than I thought."

She narrowed her eyes at me.

"You knew their plan, didn't you? And you knew they'd
screw it up somehow and be caught. But it was the perfect way
to get rid of your enemies. You let Ferdinand be the sacrifice—I
mean, he'd hurt you plenty of times, so you figured he was
deserving—and you'd let things play out naturally with them
eventually getting caught. And you get to play the helpless
victim. Marvin you didn't plan for, but there's not much you can
do about that now. But Chuckles, he caught them that night,
didn't he? He didn't know why they were setting Ferdinand up
to die, but he was going to do something about it. So you had to
kill him."

Her face softened and a slight grin played across her lips.
"As long as he had a bottle of something hard waiting for him in
his trailer, Chuckles was happy. And every night, after we'd
finished up for the day, he'd go straight to his trailer and drink

until he passed out. The likelihood of him catching them was a thousand to one. I was checking on them that night to make sure things were going according to their plan, when I spotted him stumbling into the big top. He was drunk, but not so drunk that he didn't understand exactly what they were up to. I waited for them to see him, but they never did. Further proof that they were too stupid to pull it off alone. He wandered out of the tent and I followed him to see where he was going. Once we reached your building, I saw the police station just up the street and I knew he was going to turn them in." Her hands shook as she tightened her robe around herself. "So I had to kill him. He left me no choice."

"The weapon—" Harper started.

"I grabbed it from my trailer before I went to spy on them that night. Ironically, it's the same one Lucky used to kill Marvin." She smirked.

"Why did you stuff the flyer in his mouth though?" I asked.

She shrugged a single shoulder. "I actually saw it lying on the ground and it seemed like a nice clue to plant. I thought it would make it appear that someone from our circus had done it in a fit of rage."

"Curly is going to be devastated," I thought out loud.

Her eyes darted in my direction. "Curly will understand why I did what I did. And he will honor the Braun name as he rebuilds the circus my father first built all those years ago."

Harper placed a gentle hand around Elsa's arm and spoke in his radio to Dobson, who had just arrived to help Coralee.

"Should I get Curly?" I asked.

Elsa shook her head. "No, he's already seen his mother arrested once today." She lowered her head and let Harper lead her away.

Dorothy put her arm around my shoulders. "I always knew you were smart." She smiled at me. "And now I've had a front row seat to you solving a murder!" She gave me a squeeze, "What an eventful day we've had."

"Yes, and I'm exhausted. Let's get out of here."

CHAPTER 20

*H*arper and Dobson stood on either side of Elsa as they walked to Dobson's cruiser and I watched them chatting as Dorothy and I walked a few yards behind them. Dobson kept shooting me strange looks over his shoulder and I wondered if he'd somehow forgotten that he'd seen Harper shift into a fox. Call me crazy, but I felt like me turning people into chickens wasn't the weirdest thing he saw that day.

"Granny disappeared today," I said.

"What do you mean?" Dorothy brought her hand to her chest.

"After I did that spell or whatever on Ridley. She disappeared."

"That's odd," Dorothy said, her feet crunching the gravel beneath them. "You know, she can be a tough nut to crack, she's not good with sharing her feelings, and she can certainly be a bit insufferable at times, but there's no one else I'd rather have in my corner." Dorothy bumped me with her shoulder and gave me a knowing smile.

"Didn't anyone ever tell you it's not nice to gossip?" Granny's voice came from behind us and I whirled around.

"There you are! Why did you disappear like that?"

"You scared me." She shrugged.

"What do you mean?"

"I'll just give you two a moment," Dorothy said before she started walking toward Harper and Dobson again.

"Dru, what you did back there—you shouldn't have been able to do that. There's no way you should've been able to do that. And I admit, it scared me."

"But why would that scare you? I don't understand."

"The more power you have, the more dangerous things can be for you. I don't know if you're ready for all that yet." She adjusted her glasses. "I know I'm not."

"Do we really have a choice?"

"Ha. No." She smiled. "No, I guess we don't."

I started walking again, taking my time and thinking about the events of the day.

"Granny, my grandfather—"

"Not this again. Please." She groaned.

"*I* guess I just don't really understand why you're so averse to talking about him."

"Oh, Dru," she sighed, "we all have that one. Elsa had Ferdinand. And Marvin, it seems. Poor thing. You had Jason. And I had your grandfather."

"Jason was *not* the one." I said, offended that she'd dare say such a thing.

"I didn't say *the* one. I said *that* one. You know, the man you think is your knight in shining armor and then you wake up one day and realize he's just a jackass wielding a plastic butter knife and wrapped in tin foil. That one."

I laughed.

"Look, the sooner you accept that it had nothing to do with you and everything to do with him, the sooner you can move on and find happiness again."

"Granny, no offense, but you still refuse to talk about your ex from like, fifty years ago. And you never remarried or anything, did you?"

"No, but that was my happiness. And what happened to me was different. We were married and we had a baby and he decided having magic was more important than us. I'm not going to minimize what happened to you, but you have to realize that the betrayal I experienced was a lot deeper."

"Did he have his magic when you met him?" I asked.

She let out a long sigh. "I might as well let all the cats out of the bag. Your grandfather was my guardian, Dru."

I gasped.

"And then he decided that he wanted magic for himself. Being a shapeshifter wasn't enough for him. He wanted power. He became obsessed with it. Almost to the point of madness. He finally got what he was after, and then one day, he was just gone."

"Wow. Granny, that's terrible. I'm so sorry." I wished I could give her a hug.

"Good riddance," she said, disgusted. "Look, I don't want you to suffer like I did. Spending most of your life cynical and thinking the only good men are the dead ones. Not all men are Jason. Or Lucian, for that matter."

I shook my head. "I really don't understand you. You've been beating into my head that Harper is off limits. Not just you, but everyone. My dad is really against it, Mom too, and the coven makes passive aggressive comments sometimes. And I get it. I do. After what happened to my mom and now that I know your experience with having a relationship with your Guardian ended badly... I mean, it all makes sense. But you—you're always straightforward with me. It's never a secret where you stand. So why are you being so wishy-washy about this?"

"I'm not." She shrugged.

"Yes, you are. The whole 'we have rules, Dru' business. But then you say things about finding my happiness and all that and I don't know what in the heck I'm supposed to do!"

"Well, are you a rule breaker or not?" She asked in an even tone. Well, that was unexpected.

"What?" I asked.

"Dru." She sighed. "We have rules, yes. And as your grandmother who loves you, I want you to be safe. I want you to live a long and fairly uneventful life, if I'm being honest. So do I push the rules that will keep you safe? Of course I do. How could I not? But that doesn't mean that I don't understand where you're coming from. And it doesn't mean that I don't want you to be happy. I do. And it doesn't mean that I won't support you in making your own decisions."

I was touched, but I didn't know how to respond.

"Follow your heart and see where it leads you," she said.

"I know. It's just...I'm scared."

"So be scared. But you do it anyway." She wagged her finger at me.

"Thanks, Granny." I smiled. "You're a pretty smart old lady."

"Pfft." She made a dismissive noise. "By the way, 'reverse the curse'?"

"What?" I feigned offense.

She let out a mocking laugh. "That was maybe the dumbest spell I've ever heard."

"Hey!" I narrowed my eyes at her but couldn't hide the smile on my face, "It's not like you were helping. And I don't have any spells memorized. So I decided to just, I don't know, wing it." I chuckled.

"Yeah, you definitely need to do some studying. Learn Latin. Hardly anyone knows it anymore so it's perfect. That way if your incantation is stupid it will at least sound respectable. Even if you don't know what you're doing, it will sound like you do."

"Thanks for the tip." I said, just as we came upon Dorothy who had stopped to wait for me.

"I love you," I whispered to Granny.

"Ew. Don't get all sappy on me. Save that for someone else," she said.

"You ready?" Harper called out, walking back toward us from the street. I watched Dobson's cruiser drive off behind him, Elsa sitting in the backseat for the second time that day.

"Go on." Dorothy smiled. "I'll catch up with you. I can manage to walk on my own just fine. And Granny's here, right? I'll just talk her ear off. It'll be nice to tell her a story for once without having to listen to her smart remarks."

Granny groaned. "No thanks. I'm just going to go. Don't tell her though," she said before vanishing.

I nodded and quickened my pace to catch up with Harper, but I heard Dorothy start telling a story about her most recent trip to the supermarket and how incensed she'd been with the price of avocados.

Harper greeted me with a smile as I linked my arm through his.

"I'm glad we made up," I said, feeling the warmth of him next to me as a light breeze from the bay picked up.

"Me too."

"I'm so ready for things to get back to normal." I rested my head on his shoulder, enjoying the peace of the moment.

"Do you even know what normal is?" He chuckled. We reached his cruiser and he opened the passenger door for me. Just as I was about to step in, I saw Trixie and Chuckles again, standing across the street.

Trixie waved in her usual fashion, a huge smile on her face. Chuckles held up a hand and mouthed the words 'thank you.' And before I knew it, they were gone. I settled myself in Harper's car and we sat in easy silence while we waited for Dorothy to catch up.

"*T*hink they'll be okay? Ridley and Curly, I mean," I asked.

"I hope so." Harper grabbed my hand and gave it a reassuring squeeze.

I watched the big top's flag blowing in the wind

CHAPTER 21

"Thank you so much, ladies," I mumbled through a mouthful of pizza.

Eve had said they weren't technically fairies, but they certainly looked like every description of a fairy that I'd ever heard. I mean, they had wings and everything.

I sat cross-legged on the couch in leggings and an old paint-splattered T-shirt and watched them zoom around the room while I stuffed my face with a breakfast of cold, leftover pizza. I tried to count how many there were, but they weren't much bigger than my hand and they flitted around so quickly that it was hard to keep track.

There was one that obviously fancied herself the leader. She wasn't the oldest, but she was certainly the bossiest. She stopped in front of me, hovering above my open pizza box and fluttering her wings. "Well, we're done here. Just finishing up the last bit."

I knew I was gawking, but I couldn't help it. I was still in awe.

"What?" She placed her hands on her hips.

"Oh, nothing," I stuttered, "I just… so you're witches? Tiny little witches. Is that right?" I leaned back and wiped my mouth with the back of my hand.

She fluttered a few inches closer and squinted at me, "Yeah, we're witches. We're not *that* tiny though. What's so hard to understand?" Her voice was ten octaves too high but it was intimidating, nonetheless.

"Nothing." I shook my head. Cleaning fairies were one of the best things that had ever happened to me and I wasn't about to let my big mouth ruin it for me already.

"Fiona says we're all squared up." She eyed me carefully, "See ya next time." And with that she zoomed away and joined a flurry of vibrantly colored flying witches as they made their way out of an open window.

"I see it didn't take you long to solicit their services." I hadn't noticed Granny had appeared and was standing in the kitchen.

I wiped my hands on my leggings and stood, carrying the empty pizza box and setting it on the kitchen counter next to the sink.

I opened the refrigerator door and took out a can of soda. "All right. Spill it." I bumped the refrigerator door closed with my hip and cracked open the can.

"Spill what?" She asked.

"Did you just get in?" I glanced at the time on the microwave. "You're coming in later and later. I think I might need to instill a curfew." I teased.

She rolled her eyes at me and waved a dismissive hand.

"Come on. Tell me where you've been going every night." I took a drink of my soda and felt the carbonation burn my throat.

"Why are you so worried about it?"

I groaned. "Granny, come on. I'm dying to know. Especially because you're making such a big deal about not telling me. *Please.*" I begged.

"Fine." She sighed.

I held my breath in anticipation.

"I was at a party." She finally answered.

"A party?" I said in disbelief.

"Yes, a party." She adjusted her glasses.

"Granny, what kind of party is an eighty-year-old ghost going to three nights in a row?" I asked in a skeptical tone.

"There's a hotel in town. One of Cheris Sterling's places, believe it or not."

Cheris Sterling owned every hotel, motel, inn — and any other type you can think of — in all of Blackwood Bay and she had been a thorn in my family's side since my mother and her were children. She'd also attempted to steal Granny's building out from under me when I'd first arrived in Blackwood Bay.

"You stepped foot in one of Cheris Sterling's establishments?" I was shocked.

"Well, you did always say over your dead body." My mom joked.

"Do you want to hear the story or not?" Granny asked in a clipped tone.

"Oh boy, do we." Maui chimed in, settling himself on the kitchen counter between us.

"I went out for a little walk one night after you'd gone to bed—"

"A walk?" I interrupted.

"Fine. I was on my way to play a few little tricks on Dorothy and Minnie. You know, just some fun ghostly pranks.

It's harmless." She waved her hand, "But that's beside the point. Anyway, so I was out and I saw the hotel just lit up like a Christmas tree inside. I could see people dancing and having a grand old time. And then I realized they were ghosts. Just like me." She pointed at her chest.

"A ghost party?" I scrunched up my face.

"Yup." She nodded. "So I went in and you know... had some fun for once."

"Sorry we don't keep you well entertained." I teased.

"I get bored, you know. I don't sleep. I don't eat. And the only ones I ever get to talk to are you three."

"And we are a delight." Maui purred.

"So tell us about this ghost party that was so amazing that you just *had* to attend three nights straight." My mom said.

"Oh, it was like something out of a movie." Her eyes widened, "It was so lavish and there was music and dancing all night long. I felt like I'd walked straight into the 1920s with the way everyone was talking and the getups they had on. It was almost magical."

"That sounds amazing. Oh! Take me with you next time?" I held my hands up like I was pleading.

"I won't be going back." She knit her brow together.

"Why?" My mom asked.

"Probably banned." Maui said in a low voice.

"I wasn't banned." She shot him a look. "Something is... off about it."

"What do you mean?"

"Well, it took awhile before it occurred to me but some of them... I don't think they could see me." She adjusted her glasses out of habit.

"Are you sure they were ghosts then?" I asked.

"Right. Are you sure you didn't intrude on some poor living person's party?" Maui tilted his head to the side.

"No." She rolled her eyes. "They weren't living people. They were ghosts. And it wasn't all of them that couldn't see me. I've never experienced that before with spirits. I don't quite know how to explain it other than something wasn't right. It just gave me a bad feeling."

"Interesting." I traced my finger around the lid of my soda can.

"Don't get any ideas. I told you I'm not going back. It *is* Cheris Sterling's hotel after all. It wouldn't surprise me if I got a bad vibe because the gate to hell was hidden in there somewhere." She joked.

I let out a laugh. "All right. Case closed then. We'll just leave it as an unsolved mystery."

She opened her mouth to say something else but there was a light rap on the front door.

I hurried to check myself out in the large, ornate mirror hanging in the living room. That's the problem with unexpected company. They never show up when you're all dolled up. It's always when you're having a lazy day eating cold pizza and lounging on the couch in leggings watching tiny little witches clean your apartment. Another knock, a bit louder this time, startled me.

"It's your bloke." Maui said, peering out the window in the kitchen.

It was Harper? Great.

"Coming!" I called out.

I threw my unwashed hair up in a messy bun on top of my head and wiped at a speck of pizza sauce on my chin before padding in my bare feet across the floor. I threw the door open more enthusiastically than I had intended.

"Hi." He took a step back.

"Hi." I shifted my weight to one foot and tried to nonchalantly lean against the open door, fumbling to figure out where to put my hand.

I heard snickering behind me.

Harper gave me a quick once over.

"Cleaning day." I tugged at the hem of my stained T-shirt.

"Oh, no," he held up a hand and widened his eyes. "It's cute. You look cute." His cheeks turned a light shade of pink.

I felt mine grow hot.

"Mercy." Granny muttered.

"Uh, anyway," he rubbed the back of his neck, "I wanted to stop by and check on you this morning."

"Thanks. I'm doing okay." I smiled and hoped I didn't have any food stuck in my teeth. "By the way, how's Dobson? I asked Tilly to come by and perform a memory spell on him and the circus performers you took in yesterday."

He chuckled. "Well, he's fine now. It was a little dicey for awhile there. He had a lot of questions. Tilly was waiting for him when he brought Elsa in last night. For the second time."

"Well, we can always count on her. She loves performing memory spells more than anyone I know." I let out a little laugh.

"Good. Great." He smiled and looked around like he was trying to work up the nerve to say what came next.

"Spit it out, mate." I heard Maui mumble as he bounced from the kitchen counter and onto the couch.

"I was just thinking, and let me know if this is... I don't know, inappropriate or something." He shrugged. "Um, but I was just thinking maybe sometime we could – I don't know – catch a movie or eat dinner some place that forces me to wear a tie... or not — maybe just grab coffee and take a walk on the beach? Or, do you like boats? Carver has a boat—"

"Harper." I cut him off.

"Thank you. Jeez. Put the man out of his misery." Granny quipped.

He gave me a sheepish look and bit his lower lip.

"Yes, I'd love to." I tried to keep an even tone despite my heart feeling like it might pound right through my chest.

"Really?" He raised his eyebrows in surprise.

"Yes, of course. I had a lot of fun with you the other night. Well, right up until everything went sideways. But before that it was great."

"Okay, awesome." He was grinning like the Cheshire cat. "Great." He started towards the steps but turned back suddenly, "Oh! I forgot. I wanted to let you know I stopped by the circus again this morning."

"Oh yeah?"

He nodded, "I wanted to see how they were holding up after everything that's happened the last couple of days. Curly was having a pretty hard time coming to terms with his mother being a murderer, but they seem to have figured out a plan."

"What's the plan then?"

"Curly's the owner now, technically, and he'll be the new ringmaster. I didn't know this but his grandfather, Elsa's dad, was a little person too. Curly really wants to try to get back to their roots. Everyone else seems to be on board and from what I gathered, Ridley will be the brains of the new operation."

"What about Coralee?"

"He's letting her stay. I think Ridley talked him into it, actually."

I felt my eyes widen. "So they're just going to continue on as if nothing happened?"

"Sounds like it. In fact, they're heading out today and moving onto their next scheduled stop."

"Wow." I paused, "Well, as they say, the show must go on, right?" I shrugged.

He grinned and gave me a wink. "Circus folk."

The End

ABOUT THE AUTHOR

Misty Bane is a Pacific Northwest native currently living somewhere between the mountains and the beach with her husband, three children, and golden retriever, Lou. She often fantasizes about living in a world where she could clean the house and whip up a four-course meal with just a twirl of her finger.

Keep up with Misty by following her on social media. To be notified of new releases and special discounts, join her newsletter list. She has a strict anti-spam policy and you will never receive anything you didn't sign up for.

You can also join her Facebook Reader Group.

ACKNOWLEDGMENTS

There are so many people that work behind the scenes and these stories would never see the light of day without them.

My Family, thank you for your support and encouragement always.

My amazing ARC Team. You all are the best team an author could ever ask for.

An extra special huge thank you to Misha for being so generous with her time and awesome proofreading skills.

And finally, my readers. Thank you for reading my stories. I sincerely appreciate each and every one of you!

Made in the
USA
Lexington, KY